Battle for the Park

Battle for the Park

Park

COLIN DANN

HUTCHINSON

London Sydney Auckland Johannesburg

First published in 1992 by Hutchinson Children's Books
an imprint of the Random Century Group Ltd
20 Vauxhall Bridge Road, London SW1V 2SA

Random Century Australia (Pty) Ltd
20 Alfred Street, Milsons Point, Sydney, NSW 2061, Australia

Random Century New Zealand Ltd
PO Box 40–086, Glenfield, Auckland 10, New Zealand

Random Century South Africa (Pty) Ltd
PO Box 337, Bergvlei, 2012 South Africa

Printed in Great Britain by
Butler & Tanner Ltd., Frome, Somerset

Phototypeset by Intype, London

British Library Cataloguing in Publication Data is available.
ISBN 0 09 176425 4

Contents

In fond memory of a great friend, John Goodchild, who was the first to risk publishing me, this book is dedicated with my deepest gratitude.

— 1 —

Fox and Hare

Plucky the young fox and Dash the yearling hare were firm friends. They had grown up together in the corner of White Deer Park Nature Reserve where the animals from Farthing Wood had settled and brought up their young. Plucky was a direct descendant of the Farthing Wood Fox who, though now elderly, was still active and living with his beloved Vixen in the same earth they had always used. As for Dash, she was the daughter of a hare who had travelled the long journey from Farthing Wood as a tiny leveret and who, because of this, had always been known as Leveret by his friends. For a while Dash had stood a little in awe of Plucky on account of his illustrious ancestor. She had been too shy and wary to join in his frolics. But after her first winter she grew bolder and began to accompany him on his rambles. She was very frisky and liked to dart about, enjoying the power and speed her long legs gave her.

She knew she was perfectly safe with Plucky. Amongst the Farthing Wood community, fox and hare could be friends and, besides, none of its predator animals, fox or otherwise, ever hunted in the home area of the Park. This was how it had always been, ever since the animals first settled near the Hollow where the elders gathered periodically to meet.

One beautiful sunny day in late April Plucky and Dash went gambolling together. 'Race me,' Dash challenged the fox, 'over the grass to the leaning pine.'

'I never go near leaning trees,' Plucky answered. 'After the great storm, you can never be sure when they might fall.'

'Oh, all right then,' Dash said impatiently, twitching her long silky ears, 'you say where.' Her hind feet shifted nervously, she was so eager to be off.

'See the gorse bush? Let's make it there.'

'That's not far enough,' Dash declared, her large liquid eyes glancing almost superciliously at the young fox.

'Far enough for me,' Plucky muttered.

'What about there and back again?'

'If you want to.'

'Come on then, Plucky. Ready?' Dash sprang away and galloped over the short spring grass, exhilarated by the freshness of the weather and her own pace and verve. And Plucky was no slouch at running himself. He hurtled after the young hare gleefully and, because Dash was averse to running in a straight line and instinctively swerved and deviated from her course, now bearing this way and now that, he managed to keep up with her as he aimed directly for the gorse bush. He soon found, however, that Dash had been toying with him. As he rounded the prickly shrub close on her tail, he saw her suddenly accelerate, as if she had decided all at once to give him an example of real speed. In no time at all, it seemed, he was watching her lithe brown-coated body disappearing into the dis-tance. He actually stopped to watch her more closely, marvelling at the smaller animal's awesome swiftness. Dash checked herself and turned to see just how far behind her Plucky was. He hastened now to catch her up. Dash looked back at her friend's efforts with a touch of disdain. Plucky made a great thing of arriving in a breathless state and he panted lavishly.

'I hope I haven't exhausted you?' Dash asked with real concern.

'Oh no,' Plucky gasped. 'But I think we may as well give up these races; they're too one-sided.'

Dash looked pleased. She began to groom herself laboriously although she was already spotless.

'What a simply wonderful runner you are,' Plucky said with admiration. 'You're as fleet as the wind and as agile as a grasshopper.' He had made up this eulogy some time before but had never got round to speaking it. Dash wasn't quite sure about the grasshopper bit but she was very flattered. Mostly she was flattered because it was Plucky who had praised her. She held him in the highest regard, and indeed throughout the Farthing Wood community he was accepted as the strongest and boldest of the young foxes, with many of the attributes of the Farthing Wood Fox when young. That she – a mere hare – should be praised by such an impressive animal! And she hadn't even fully stretched herself!

'If I could run over the downland like my father did, then I'd truly show you something,' she told her companion. 'But you're very kind to compliment me.'

'Your father? When did he run over the downland?' Plucky was puzzled.

'On the journey to White Deer Park from his old home, with *his* father and mother and the elders like Fox and Badger. He wasn't much more than a baby then.'

'Does he remember all about the journey still?'

'Yes. You'd never forget something like that, would you?'

Plucky looked away towards the Park's boundaries as though he were trying to picture what it must have

been like. But all the descendants of the original animals of Farthing Wood were familiar enough with the
story. He turned back and gave Dash a dubious look.
'I don't think you'll ever be able to exercise your speed
beyond the Reserve,' he remarked. 'The fences have
been strengthened since the hurricane and there are no
exits any more. Except for a bird,' he added with a wry
expression.

'It's not fair,' Dash complained. 'Tawny Owl and
Whistler don't have to be cooped up like we are.'

'We're not cooped up, Dash,' said Plucky firmly.
'We're protected here. And surely this Park is big
enough for you?'

Dash considered. 'To live in most of the time, yes.
But I would so love to know just how fast I can go.
However, as I haven't got wings,' she continued peev-
ishly, 'I suppose I never will.'

'But you *have* got wings,' Plucky told her. 'Wings to
your feet.'

The young hare melted at this new flattery. 'Oh,
you're a – a – smooth-tongued animal,' she said coyly.

'Maybe. But I'm no racer,' said Plucky. 'Have you
thought of challenging your father?'

'Yes. We've run together and he's no match for me.'

'What about the rabbits?'

'Rabbits? If my father can't beat me, I hardly
think – '

Plucky interrupted her. 'Have you raced against a
deer?' he asked subtly. He wanted very much for Dash
to forget any notion of testing herself beyond the safety
of the Nature Reserve.

'No, I haven't done that,' she admitted. She seemed
rather to like the suggestion. 'It could certainly be
an interesting competition. But how could I approach
them? They'd probably think I was silly.'

'I'm sure they wouldn't; but, if you like, I'll tackle them for you.'

'Would you really, Plucky? I know you're not scared of deer.'

'Scared of them? I should think not.' Plucky drew himself up. 'After the stag Trey was injured and taken away there's now no-one to fear in the herd.'

'You even stood up to *him*, didn't you?' Dash murmured wonderingly. 'D'you think he'll ever come back?'

'No, not after all this time. He must have died from the injuries he received during the storm.'

Dash was beginning to feel restless. She wanted to be moving again. 'Let's go to the Pond,' she said. 'There's often something interesting happening there.' And she bounded away.

'Wait!' cried Plucky urgently. 'Don't go that way!'

Dash checked herself and turned about. 'Why not?'

'There are men approaching,' Plucky explained. 'Look!'

Men had been noticeable around the Reserve for some months and, although the resident wild creatures were accustoming themselves to this, they still didn't care to be too close to them. Apart from the Warden, with whom all the animals were so familiar that they accepted him almost as one of themselves, the human presence had first been evident after the hurricane. Then the operation of clearing fallen or dangerous trees, repairing boundary fences and so on had meant that, in the daylight hours, a contingent of workmen was needed within White Deer Park. There had been a lot to do and, now that everything had finally reached completion, there was a different kind of work taking place. At the instigation of the Warden, the County Naturalists' Trust was conducting a population census of the chief groups of the Park's fauna. This was done every few years anyway, but now there was an additional, more pressing need. This was because, after the second mild winter in succession, all the animal groups were enjoying something of a population explosion. They had increased well beyond the levels that had existed before the last really severe winter. Beasts and birds had multiplied so much that the fact of the matter was the Reserve was becoming crowded.

But Plucky and Dash didn't know that. The young fox led his friend away from the interested humans in a circuitous route towards the Pond. The Pond had become a focal point in the Park since almost every creature now used it as its water hole. The stream that ran through the Park had been designated a dangerous place when it became infected by poisonous chemicals, and the Park's inhabitants had discovered this the hard way. Now it was avoided as a drinking place and thus the Pond was frequently busy. On this occasion, however, since it was mid-morning, few animals were about. Dash was disappointed. She had hoped to see some of the deer, at least.

'We seem to be on our own,' she commented. She watched Plucky lap messily at the water's edge. 'Where *is* everyone?'

Plucky looked up from his drink. 'Under cover, I should think.' Water trickled down his chin, forming large drops. 'I bet Toad's skulking around here, though, amongst the reeds.'

Dash didn't answer. She wasn't tremendously interested in this prospect, preferring more lively companions. But Plucky was fond of this smallest member of the Farthing Wood elders, just as he was of all of them, and went to look for him. Dash let him go. She wanted to race some more and could see that, for the present, Plucky had other ideas. She decided she wouldn't wait for the young fox to speak to the deer, she would go and do it herself now. She gave Plucky a last glance and then bounded away in search of the herd.

Toad was swimming lazily in the shallows under a fringe of rushes. He didn't venture further out these days. He was an old toad and didn't exert himself too much. He was actually contemplating the profusion of tadpoles – well-grown by now – that had hatched in the water that season. Some of them, doubtless, were his and other toads' progeny but there were others that were unmistakably those of frogs. The Edible Frog colony had grown steadily in size and the population of Common Frogs in the Park was equally thriving. All the tadpoles were voracious feeders. They seemed to be competing in outgrowing one another and the Pond was alive with their darting, wriggling little bodies.

'There can't be sufficient food for all of them,' Toad mused. 'Some of 'em are never going to make adulthood.' It was as he was brooding like this that Plucky spied him and barked a greeting.

Toad croaked in answer. 'Now then,' he went on, 'where's your playmate?'

Plucky looked a mite rueful. 'Oh well, to be honest, you know, Toad, she wears me out sometimes.'

'Yes. She makes me tired just watching her,' Toad commented. 'But how glorious it must feel to be able to run like that!' He pulled himself on to the bank. His brown wrinkly skin glistened and gleamed.

Plucky became aware of the churning of the water. 'My word!' he exclaimed, noticing the writhing mass of tadpoles. 'There's a feast going there for hungry fish.' Then, recalling suddenly with whom he was conversing, he apologized. 'I'm so sorry,' he said contritely. 'I forgot for a moment they may be your kin.'

'Quite all right, my young friend,' Toad answered

cheerily. 'I could never tell you which of them are, anyway. But, since you mention it, I can tell you there are fewer fish in here than there were, and that may partly explain this – this – multitude.'

'Fewer fish?' Plucky echoed. 'How's that?'

'The Warden's moved some of them to the stream.'

'The *stream*?' Plucky cried. 'But I thought – '

Toad interrupted. 'So Whistler says. He used to fish there, as you know, but when the poison got into the water, everything died. Now he tells me he's seen fish swimming in it once more, and so the water must be clean again. He's kept an eye on the stream all along. He says the Warden's been very busy, introducing all sorts of creatures and plants along its length.'

'Then the stream's alive again,' Plucky concluded. 'Does the heron feed there once more?'

Toad chuckled. 'Not Whistler. You know him; he's a canny old bird. He'll give it a while yet to make sure.'

'I think he's very – ' Plucky began, then broke off as he heard the rapid thump of galloping feet. He looked up sharply. Toad squatted beside him, ready to dive back into the Pond if necessary. Across the broad pool they saw a young hind, running full-tilt. Almost before they could quite make out what was happening they picked out a second blur of movement to the rear of the female deer. This materialized into the shape of a hare, which rapidly drew level with the hind and then, almost without effort, hurtled ahead, kicking up dust as it went. Dash was once again demonstrating her superiority as a racer. She galloped on round the Pond's perimeter until she was running toward Plucky.

'You see!' he and Toad heard her call. 'I'm invincible!' She arrived, braking sharply and then dancing her delight. The hind had slowed down and had turned to drink. 'There's nothing here to test me,' Dash declared. 'You saw it, Plucky. Not even a deer can offer

me real competition. Most of the hinds had their young
to tend. This one's unmated and I had to goad *her*
before she would run at all. I just shan't ever know
how good I am until I can get outside this place and
really stretch my legs.'

'Don't talk so silly,' Toad reprimanded her. 'Try and
be more sensible, Dash. You can't go out of bounds.
You'd be putting yourself at risk.'

'Pooh, what could catch *me*?' Dash scoffed airily.

'What about a gun?' Toad reminded her. He was
annoyed.

'A gun? There are no guns round here. I never hear
a gun,' she argued obstinately. She turned to Plucky.
'Oh Plucky, won't you scrape a little exit for me under
the fence somewhere, just a little shallow one? I'd only
use it once, you know, to get out and really – '

'Certainly not!' Plucky snapped. 'We're friends, you
and I, Dash, but don't expect me to be your accomplice
in such a foolhardy escapade. And besides, I want you
safe,' he added in a much softer tone.

Dash ignored the last remark. 'Oh, you've no sense
of adventure!' she derided him. 'All right then. You're
not the only one who can dig a hole. I'll simply find
someone else!' Piqued, she leapt away, flinging him a
scornful look.

'I wouldn't put it past her,' Toad grunted. 'She's a
wilful young creature.'

Plucky left the Pond anxiously. Toad urged him to
follow the hare if he could and try to talk some sense
into her.

'I'll do my best,' Plucky promised, 'though I don't
know if she'll listen to me. I've tried once already but
she's got this idea into her head. . . .' He loped away,
looking all around for a sight of his friend's bounding
brown figure. When he couldn't find her he put his

nose to the ground in an attempt to track her. It was a vain attempt. Dash, like all hares, left a zigzagging track that sometimes doubled back on itself, and it was certainly beyond Plucky's skills to follow this. He gave up the trail and, moving more slowly, headed in the direction of his home area, hoping to find Dash there.

— 2 —

Round and Round

The mild winters had been kind to Badger, who, ancient as he was, could not have withstood much harsh weather. Since the storm he had lived comfortably and contentedly in his new set close to Fox and Vixen. He was always able to find sufficient food for his needs. He had the best company he could have wished for in his two old friends and, once he had refined his set and shaped it to his liking, he didn't really miss his old home, which had been destroyed by a fallen tree during the hurricane. But Badger was puzzled and, this day, when he was talking to Fox, he mentioned his puzzlement.

'I don't understand it,' he said. 'This little wood was never like this at one time.'

Fox looked at Badger dubiously, wondering what was coming next. The old creature sometimes became confused about things. 'It was never like what?' he queried.

'Well, sort of – sort of *full*, Fox,' Badger replied. 'There was always plenty of room for everyone. You never felt crowded. You met others in the course of your wanderings or, on occasion, deliberately if you wanted to talk about something. But now . . . I never set foot outside my set without seeing a host of little animals and often bigger ones, too, such as squirrels and hedgehogs and even foxes – you'll excuse me for saying so, I know.'

Fox was amused. 'We foxes have certainly increased over the seasons. It's in the nature of things, Badger.'

'Of course it is, of course it is. I wasn't referring to your own numerous descendants,' Badger assured him. 'But just generally – there's more of everything.'

'You're quite right,' Fox agreed. 'There's a denser congregation of animals in this wood – and birds too – than when we first set up home here. But that must be a good sign, surely? It shows White Deer Park is thriving.'

'Well, yes, as long as there's enough for all of us to eat,' Badger said. 'I've had no problems so far but, if the trend continues. . . . And then, is it the same all over the Park – the numbers, I mean? I don't go far enough to know.'

'I think I could say so,' Fox answered. 'Yes, wildlife is certainly flourishing here. And, you know' – he looked thoughtful – 'I believe humans find this interesting. It seems to me they come into the Park to observe us in some way.'

Badger grunted. 'And that's another thing,' he remarked. 'In the old days there was only the Warden, and he used to keep himself to himself mostly. Men have been around here on and off ever since the storm.'

'We *do* seem to be becoming an attraction,' Fox murmured. 'I wonder if there's anything in it?'

They weren't able to ponder much on the subject just then because they saw Plucky approaching, looking agitated. The young fox ran straight up to them. 'Have you seen her?' he asked at once, rather vaguely.

'She's asleep,' Badger answered, thinking Plucky was referring to Vixen. 'Underground.'

'Underground?' Plucky repeated. 'Whatever is she up to now? She's not a rabbit!'

Fox saw there was some error. 'Who are you looking for?' he asked patiently.

'Dash, of course.'

'I guessed as much. No, we haven't seen her. You should make yourself clear, Plucky. Badger thought you were talking about Vixen.'

'I'm really worried,' Plucky gabbled on, explaining about their races and Dash's desire to stretch herself.

'Slow down, slow down.' Fox tried to cut through this outpouring. 'Now, take a breather.' He watched the youngster's efforts to calm himself. 'Good. That's better. Now, there's nothing more you can do for the present, is there? You don't know where she is. I wouldn't get my fur in a bristle over this. That's my advice. I can't think of any creature who'd be foolish enough to abet this plan of the young hare's to get out of the Reserve. Does this allay your fears?'

'I suppose so, yes.' And Plucky was comforted; Fox was so wise and experienced in things.

'And as soon as I see her,' Fox went on, 'I'll drive any such daft idea right out of her head. That's a promise.'

'So will I,' Badger echoed. 'She could come to real harm out there. Men shoot animals like her for fun.'

Plucky gulped at the thought. 'That's what Toad said,' he muttered.

Later Fox told Vixen about it all. He always discussed everything with her. 'Poor Plucky was in a state. I tried to make him feel easy,' he explained to her. 'I think he prefers the hare's company to that of his own kind, in a way. I didn't tell him what I was really thinking – that the rabbits, Dash's cousins, can tunnel. And I don't have to tell you how unpredictable *they* can be.'

'No indeed,' Vixen concurred. 'Although you and I have cause to be grateful to rabbits, haven't we? After

all, in an indirect way, they brought us together in the
first place.' She nuzzled him lovingly as they lay side
by side in their dark earth.

The pair of foxes were silent for a while. Then Vixen
said, 'I think Dash's father should be alerted. Leveret
knows all about the hazards of the downland.'

In reality the impetuous Dash soon forgot her silly
remark once she had recovered from her disappoint-
ment. She knew Plucky cared greatly for her safety,
and his concern for her made her warm to him even
more. She rejoiced in having such a friend and counted
herself lucky that he wished to protect her. She certainly had no intention of setting out perversely to upset
him. So she contented herself with tearing about the
Reserve from one side to the other and pitting herself
against any animal who felt like accepting her challenge. Rabbits were easily vanquished. Deer she had
already disposed of. Foxes were no match, she knew.
But she found other hares, apart from those in her own
family, who felt they might have the legs of her. She
soon proved them otherwise. Where they were swift,
Dash was swifter. Where they could bound, she could
vault and leap. And where they excelled, Dash could
still surpass them. Eventually she could find no new
takers and she was left to race alone, reduced to demonstrating, to the few animals who cared to notice, exactly
why no other would run with her.

She soon tired of this and wanted Plucky's com-
panionship again. And now it was her turn to go in
quest of him. However, everywhere she sought him she
drew a blank. It didn't take her elastic limbs long to
cover the whole Reserve – or at any rate all of the
Reserve that she was prepared to search, for there was
one patch that she wouldn't enter. This was a small
area, close to the perimeter fence, in which men had

recently been concentrating. She avoided this and so, unlike some of the other animals, she was blissfully ignorant of just what the group of humans had been engaged in there. Anyway, Plucky had completely disappeared and Dash, who at first thought he was steering clear of her because she had offended him, now realized his absence meant something more serious. She looked to her father for help.

'It's rare for you to stand still long enough for me to say anything to you,' Leveret commented wryly. 'What's the problem? I've heard about your longing to be out on the downland and, if it's anything to do with that, you must think again. I don't want to talk about it.'

'It's nothing to do with that,' Dash answered dismissively. 'It's Plucky. He's disappeared. I've sought him everywhere without any success. What do you think's happened?'

'I really couldn't say. Have you spoken to Fox and Vixen?'

'No, I haven't.'

'The ways of foxes are best understood by other foxes, Dash.'

'Oh yes, of course. I hadn't thought – '

'I expect,' said Leveret, 'there's some simple explanation.'

Dash was encouraged and, towards dusk, she set off for the foxes' earth.

The leaves of the copse were just beginning to unfurl. Vixen stood at the entrance to her den, sniffing the soft evening breeze. Dash came hotfoot in the gathering darkness. She quickly told Vixen her purpose.

'We don't see Plucky around as often as you might suppose,' said Vixen. 'He's a mature fox and very independent. But, the strange thing is, he was here asking about you a short while ago. You seem to be bent on avoiding each other!'

'No, no, it's not like that at all,' Dash returned. 'I did get in a bit of a huff over something with him – I know I can be a silly animal at times – but, you see, I've been looking for him all over the Park. He's just not around any more, Vixen. He's gone.'

Vixen was perturbed. 'I see,' she said quietly. 'And you've really searched everywhere?'

'Everywhere,' Dash confirmed. 'It's not like Plucky to hide himself away, is it? I'm so afraid he's been injured somewhere and can't move.'

Vixen recalled the stag Trey and how he'd been crushed by a tree. 'There are still accidents occasionally,' she murmured. 'Falling branches, loosened by the storm. Even trees, once weakened, can tumble.' She looked at Dash, whose face was a picture of misery, and regretted giving voice to her thoughts. 'I'm sorry,' she said. 'It does you credit to care for another creature so.'

'Oh dear,' Dash wailed. 'He was always so careful. He wouldn't go near a leaning tree – or – or – anything that seemed unsafe. I can't bear to think of what might have befallen him.'

'Now, don't alarm yourself unnecessarily,' Vixen said affectionately. 'We don't know anything yet. We've plenty of friends to keep their eyes open. I'll get them all to be extra vigilant, especially the birds.'

'Father says Tawny Owl is wholly absorbed these days with Holly.'

'Well, she *is* his mate,' Vixen pointed out. 'And so he's bound to give her first consideration. But he'll rally round once I've spoken to him, you'll see. He can often discover things where others can't.'

'Father says Owl's obsessed. He said he left it so late to be mated, Holly's turned his head,' Dash quoted faithfully. Vixen found it difficult to retain a serious expression. Then, thinking of an alternative, Dash said, 'What about Whistler?'

'Whistler doesn't fly so much now,' Vixen answered. 'He's a bit rheumaticky. But look, Dash, I'm glad you've brought word. Now, the best thing is for you to leave things a while. If you don't see Plucky yourself soon, or hear of him, come back to me in a few days. Fox will get things organized amongst the Farthing Wood community and I think we'll have some better news for you eventually.'

'Thank you, Vixen,' Dash said with feeling. 'You're so dependable.'

Time went on and Dash, lonely and forlorn, could bear it no longer. She returned to Vixen, almost dreading to learn of some disaster.

'It doesn't look good,' Vixen had to tell her. 'Fox and Friendly and Weasel and all the others have been out searching – even Owl. There are no new trees down. The deer herd know nothing about Plucky. It's difficult to know what more can be done.'

Dash didn't answer but she knew what she was going to do. She would go outside the Park. The idea frightened her, but she was determined about it nonetheless. She thought she could persuade one of the rabbits to help her, just as Fox had feared she would. She couldn't get the nagging thought from her head that Plucky had taken her silly threat seriously and left the Reserve in search of her, so that the two of them were going round and round looking for each other in the most hopelessly futile way. 'And if he has suffered because of me,' she told herself, 'I'll never forgive myself.'

3

In the Hollow

Dash was careful to say nothing of her intentions to anyone other than the rabbits. Even to them she didn't give her real reason for wanting to break the bounds. She invented a story about a favourite food-plant which was maddeningly just too far from the fence for her to reach, and which she craved so much that she was prepared to risk herself to get it.

'A couple of leaps and I'd be there,' she told them. 'That's all it is, that plant, a couple of leaps away.'

The rabbits, of course, were completely taken in. They knew all about favourite plants. But they would never have dared to do what Dash was proposing: they were far too timid.

'If you can scratch the soil away a little bit,' the hare said to one of the does, 'enough to enable me to squeeze under. Only take you a moment.'

And that was how Dash left the Park, the place that had been her only home since birth, and found herself on the wide and dauntingly open expanse of downland.

The Farthing Wood community was soon aware that now Dash was missing as well as Plucky, and most of them believed there was a connection. However, about the same time, other animals also began to disappear, such as squirrels, hedgehogs and rabbits. The elders arranged to meet in the Hollow. They were puzzled and alarmed by the turn of events and could find no solution to it.

'Odd that I should have remarked on how crowded our copse was,' Badger said. 'Now it's almost as if its inhabitants are being deliberately thinned out.'

'Its not solely in our corner that it's happening,' Leveret told them. 'I've heard from rabbits and hares elsewhere. They're *all* missing relatives and acquaintances.'

'Wherever can they be going?' asked Weasel. 'Where are they all, the missing ones?'

Mossy, the little mole, who was not an elder but who often visited Badger and so was included in the gatherings, said tremulously, 'They're being h-hunted. The Great Cat has come back. What else can it be? Oh! Oh! The Great Cat has returned!'

'Hush, Mole,' said Badger kindly. 'This is no hunter. No one animal could account for such losses.'

'You mean there's a pack of them?' Mossy squeaked in fright. 'Then how can any of us survive?'

'Of course he doesn't mean that,' Tawny Owl said irritably. 'Don't be absurd. One great hunter was certainly clever at hiding himself away but how could a whole gang of them remain invisible?'

The timid Mossy retreated. Weasel said of Owl, 'His pairing with Holly doesn't seem to have smoothed his feathers, does it?'

Tawny Owl bent down from his branch above the Hollow and replied angrily, 'What my mate has or hasn't done for me is none of your business, Weasel!'

'Here we go again,' drawled Adder, who up until then had remained silent.

'Oh, for goodness' sake don't start, you two,' Fox cried, addressing Owl and Weasel. 'We're here to talk constructively.'

'Well then, let's do it,' Adder lisped. 'We don't appear to know why certain residents of the Park have vanished. So the obvious thing to do is to find out before any more of us go missing. Equally, if creatures have disappeared, they must have disappeared *to* somewhere. Now where could that be?'

'Where do you suggest?' Weasel queried archly.

'Fox is the brains of the party,' Adder replied.

'I rather think the birds are our main hope here,' said Fox. 'Owl, Whistler, if you could perhaps scout around a bit you might discover something.'

'I'm afraid I'd be of little use to you, Fox,' Whistler answered ruefully. 'I really can't fly any sort of distance these days. The old wonky wing is giving me gyp; so much so I can't even feed myself properly. I've been subsisting on slugs and snails and they're really not my type of fare. The slime content alone could – '

'I think we get the picture,' Tawny Owl cut in impatiently. 'And it's no use looking to me, all of you. I'm fully committed to Holly now. My freelance days are over.'

'You mean you do her bidding,' muttered Weasel, who believed Owl's mate bossed the bird around.

Tawny Owl glared at him but didn't rise to the bait.

'Look,' said Friendly, Fox's son, 'We're not getting very far.' He turned to his father. 'Shall I see if I can pick up a clue or two?'

'Certainly,' Fox agreed. 'You know, I have a feeling that there's an element of human intervention in this business. And if that's the case it may well be something quite out of our control.'

'It couldn't be anything to do with rats, I suppose?' Toad questioned idly.

All eyes focused on the little fellow. 'Rats?' they chorused. 'What rats?'

'The rats in the Park, of course,' said Toad. He

looked around. His friends' faces mostly were blank. 'Surely you've seen them?'

'I've killed one or two in my time,' said Tawny Owl. 'So has Holly. What of it?'

'Well, I don't have to tell you that rats can carry disease. If there is disease in the Park, *that* could be the reason for animals disappearing.'

'What do *you* know about these rats, Owl?' Fox asked. 'You've said nothing on the subject before.'

'I haven't needed to,' Tawny Owl justified himself pompously. 'They weren't around in sufficient numbers to cause a problem.'

'You mean they are now?'

'I don't know,' Tawny Owl replied. 'There are more of them about now than there used to be, but – '

'Where do you see them?' Fox interrupted.

'Oh – um, well, you could see them anywhere,' the bird informed him vaguely.

'Well, *I* haven't,' Fox declared. He glanced at Vixen for corroboration.

'Neither have I,' she concurred. The other animals said the same.

'They come to the Pond now and then,' said Toad. 'They like to drink the water. But, as Owl pointed out, you could see them just about anywhere. They're very adaptable, they can eat pretty well anything, and they set up their homes where they choose. There are more coming in all the time from outside the Reserve.'

'It sounds like a kind of invasion,' Leveret remarked.

'Is this correct, Owl?' Fox appealed to him. 'What Toad's been saying?'

'Well, yes, in a way. There do seem to be more arriving. I've actually seen them climbing the fence on the town side of the Park. And of course they can tunnel in too.'

'Why on earth have you said nothing before?' Fox demanded.

'I thought you knew. And besides, Fox, what can we do about it? A few rats are not going to affect our way of life very much except to provide the predators amongst us with more food.'

'What absolute nonsense,' Fox said. 'I'm surprised at you. Of course they'll make a difference. Apart from the hazard of spreading disease, they're a threat to us. They have voracious appetites – any creature knows that. And they're predators themselves: they can eat eggs and young birds and so on. Also they're fierce animals. If we let them establish colonies here, we could all of us end up being overrun.'

There was a stunned silence. None of the animals had realized their beloved Park was at risk. Vixen was the first to break the silence. 'Humans don't like rats,' she said. 'They'll have been keeping an eye on things.'

'I wouldn't count on it,' said Toad pessimistically. 'Rats are very cautious, careful beasts. They're not going to show themselves to human eyes.'

'Toad's right,' said Weasel. 'We'll have to deal with this menace ourselves.'

'There's only one way to do that,' Fox said grimly. 'Kill them. Kill them whenever we see them and wherever we can. We shouldn't underestimate the danger, my friends. If disease enters the Park every creature, from the tiniest mouse to the largest stag in the deer herd, is in peril. We need to harness the help of every predator and every large animal in the Reserve. This could be the gravest situation White Deer Park has ever faced.'

Fox's warning, deliberately calculated, had shaken the Farthing Wood community. The elders had collected merely to discuss Dash and Plucky but had discovered once more that they needed to band together to fight for not only their homes, but their very existence. Toad was satisfied he had done his duty. He was in no position to fight anything and neither was Mossy. Fighting and slaying was a matter for animals bigger than they. Their only task now was to keep on the look-out and to report any sightings in good time to the others.

So far the influx of rats was moderate. Fox, however, deemed there was no time to be lost in gathering support from the other animals in the Reserve for his campaign of annihilation. Around White Deer Park the word was passed to other foxes, badgers, stoats and weasels. Hedgehogs and squirrels were required to play their part. Hawks and hunting birds of all sizes were tipped off by Whistler. Even the deer were brought in. Their size and weight, if nothing else, made them suitable allies in the campaign. So the Park inhabitants were primed to take action. All were ready and, for a while, the threat seemed to recede. Then, during a spell of very rainy weather, rats began to be spotted everywhere. They came over the fences, they dug under the fences. Their homes outside the Park were flooded in the downpours and they were looking for new, more secure sites. The attraction of the Reserve, where the enemy Man was scarcely in evidence, was like a magnet to the hungry, dispossessed rats. More and more came to join their fellows – big brown rats with long skinny tails, fast, purposeful, skilful and highly intelligent. The residents of the Park observed the nocturnal incursions and realized that all of them truly had a battle to face.

4

Dash's Return

Weasel was the next animal to disappear. His friends, intent on their efforts to keep the rats at bay, didn't notice his absence for a while. Eventually, as they met together in little groups, they observed Weasel was never among them. The realization that he had gone missing came as a severe blow. Weasel was one of the stalwarts of the original group of animals from Farthing Wood. He had played a part in every adventure that had befallen them. Along with Fox and Vixen, Badger, Tawny Owl, Adder and Toad, he had formed the core of the Farthing Wood community. The others felt his loss in a way that was matched only by Tawny Owl's flight from the Reserve the previous season when the bird had gone to seek a mate. But Owl had come back. None of them felt confident about Weasel's return. He had suffered the same fate as Plucky and Dash, whatever that fate was. And now the rest of them began to wonder which of their number would go next.

'You should stay near your homes,' Badger advised them, 'like I do. No strange fate can overtake those who don't wander.'

'You stay put because you have to,' said Owl. 'Your extreme age makes it so.'

'You're no fledgling yourself,' Badger reminded him.

'You sound just like Holly,' was the bird's revealing

reply. 'I mean,' he hastily added, 'she doesn't like me to overexert myself.'

'That's exactly what I'm hinting at,' Badger affirmed. 'Stay close to your roost. Let the younger ones take their turn.'

'You have a point, Badger,' Tawny Owl had the grace to admit. 'Weasel always had a habit of darting about, first here, then there, hardly able to keep still. Maybe he's paying the price now for being too active, poor creature.'

Adder couldn't restrain his usually sardonic temperament. 'I'm sure you miss him greatly,' he said with a leer.

Dash had come to no harm out on the downland. She had made her form in the new grasses and, flattening herself into its depression, had been all but invisible to prying human eyes. In the evenings she continued her search for Plucky, and her ramblings – or rather, in her case, racings – went on far into the night. She saw neither hide nor hair of him. At length she was forced to give up. She didn't care for the proximity of humans and, separated from the comfort of her friends, she felt her isolation. She wanted to be back in the Park.

Early one morning she ran back to the scrape under the boundary fence. This spot had been well used since Dash had first left the Park. She noticed there was a trampled look to the soil surface here but, since she was unaware of the invading rats, she had no explanation for it. She breathed a sigh of relief as she pulled herself into the Reserve but she was conscious of her failure in the task she had set herself. She hardly dared hope that Plucky would have returned to his old haunts in the meantime. She longed for news of him and headed directly for Fox and Vixen's earth.

The hare hadn't travelled far into the Park when she

noticed a small group of men in her path. Something about the attitude of these humans alarmed her. She veered and doubled back, then set off again on a different route. Normally she would have avoided them altogether but this time she felt compelled to return, approaching the men from behind. She was curious to discover why they were strung out at intervals in a line as though intent on barring the progress of any creature in the vicinity. She was very cautious. She hid herself behind a clump of purple honesty. She sniffed the air. She could detect the smell of other animals, although she could see none. She could hear animal noises – muffled but distinctly nervous and frightened cries. Where were these creatures? She looked about her. A motor vehicle belonging to the men stood at some distance, parked on a flat piece of ground. Dash's huge ears picked up the sounds from that quarter. She flicked her ears anxiously. The animals were inside the van! What was happening? She dared not move but she could see the van was open at the back. Inside there was an assortment of containers – boxes, crates and the like, with wire-mesh sides. From where she sat, quivering with agitation, these containers looked to Dash to be harmless examples of the kind of objects that humans always seemed to carry around with them. She didn't understand what they were. But she did understand the animal cries – cries of fear and helplessness. Then she noticed a little ripple of movement inside one of the boxes – just a flash, but unmistakable. Then in another . . . and another . . . and she knew then beyond any doubt that there were animals trapped inside them. Trapped by these very humans who were now poised ready to catch others as they ran across their path.

Dash backed away and turned to make her escape. But before she could do so she saw another creature captured. And she also saw the cunning of the humans at work. She hadn't noticed – just as none of the captured animals had noticed – that in front of the line of men was a net, camouflaged and coloured to confuse unsuspecting wildlife, and half obscured by shrubs and bushes. Now other humans hidden elsewhere began to shout and make a noise. An animal was driven from cover – this time a rabbit. Frightened and panicking, it blundered unwittingly into the folds of the net, entangling itself instantly. Before it could get free one of the men pounced and held it fast. Another came with a sack, into which the animal was stowed before being transferred to one of the containers inside the van. Dash saw a second rabbit taken and then a smaller animal, which could have been a squirrel but whose capture was so swift it was impossible for her to be sure of its identity.

She had seen enough. She was horrified by the scene. How many poor beasts had lost their liberty this way? And were there bands of humans all over the Park doing the same thing? The loss of Plucky could at last, perhaps, be explained. Groups of men had been around the Reserve for a long time. The group she had witnessed was operating in the daytime, but there could equally well be others working by night, when those animals with nocturnal habits could be rounded up: animals like badgers, hedgehogs, stoats, weasels . . . and foxes. Dash pelted full speed across the Park to the Farthing Wood animals' corner. She had to warn them to beware and now she feared to discover what other losses had taken place in her absence. Her mind was in a whirl. Animals had always been safe from human interference in White Deer Park. What was going on? How could this be happening under the nose of the Warden? *Their* Warden, the animals' Warden, whom all creatures trusted? How could these events occur without his knowledge? Was he somehow involved in them?

Dash burst into Fox and Badger's little wood. It was broad daylight so none of the foxes was about. Badger snored comfortably in his set, having dined richly on earthworms and beetle grubs. Dash heard the reverberations with frustration. Was there no-one around she could tell her news to? She thought about Plucky – removed from the Park, then taken to a strange place . . . and for what? She dared not think about that. She shuddered. Who knew what had happened to him by now? Oh, it was unbearable to think she would never see him and frolic with him again. She needed to unburden herself. She began to call, in the first place for Vixen.

After a while Vixen appeared at her earth's entrance, blinking sleepily. 'What – what is it? Who called me?'

'I did,' Dash said. 'Vixen, I have to – '

'It's you!' Vixen cried. 'We'd given you up. Where have you been? We thought you were lost, like the others.'

Dash gasped. Were there more gone? 'The – others?'

'Plucky and Weasel.'

'Is my father – '

'He's safe. So far. Now tell me, Dash, what you've found out.'

The young hare panted out all she knew. She explained hurriedly about her stay on the open downland and what she had almost stumbled into on her return. 'It's the men, Vixen! The men are taking the animals!'

Vixen was shocked. She didn't understand how such a situation could have arisen in a protected nature reserve. 'I'll speak to Fox,' she whispered.

Fox's sleep was interrupted. He emerged promptly

from the den and gave himself a good shake. 'Right,' he said. 'Tell me everything, Dash. Vixen's confused.'

Dash went over her story again, describing as clearly as she could what she had seen.

'The animals are being *trapped*?' Fox barked. 'But this can't be so. This is a wildlife sanctuary.' He racked his brains. 'There's a reason for this, there's got to be.' He turned to Vixen. 'Do you think the animals are being removed for their own safety?'

'How can anywhere be safer than here?' she questioned. 'Outside the Reserve is all hostile country.'

'The thought has occurred to me,' said Fox in a low voice, 'that there could be some danger from the rats. Supposing they are infecting other animals in some way, the Warden would need to take steps on our behalf.'

'He'd be more likely to get rid of the rats,' was Vixen's opinion. She sounded very sure on the point.

'I dare say you're right,' Fox allowed. 'Then what can it be?'

Dash knew nothing about rats. She begged the foxes to explain to her.

'Brown rats are infiltrating the Park,' Fox informed her. 'In dribs and drabs so far, but their numbers are increasing. We've been trying to keep them in check.'

Dash suddenly recalled Vixen's mention of Weasel. 'Has poor Weasel disappeared?'

'Yes, he's gone,' said Fox. He looked hard at Dash, as if all at once the implication had hit him. Weasel captured by humans! He couldn't go along with this – he, Fox, the leader of the Farthing Wood community! 'Tell me where you saw the group of men,' he snapped urgently.

Dash jumped. She was startled. 'It was – it was – as I came past the deer pasture,' she explained. 'The men were standing in a line by the rough grass. There were no deer about. Perhaps they've gone too?'

'No. I don't think so,' Fox said. 'They may have been drinking. Vixen,' he went on, 'I think we should go without delay. Dash can go with us. We have to find out where the animals are being taken. Plucky and Weasel must be rescued!'

5

In Human Hands

Fox and Vixen ran silently in Dash's wake. Less swift
than they once were, they frequently fell far behind the
hare's rapid pace. Every so often Dash paused until
they caught her up. Then, as she neared the spot where
the trap for the animals had been laid, she slowed up.
The men were no longer standing in a line. Their work
was finished for the moment and they were packing up,
bundling their equipment into the back of the van –
along with the collection of animals taken that morning.
The van was closed up. Two men got into the front.
The van's engine was started and then the vehicle
moved slowly away over the grass at a pace calculated
not to jolt the cargo. The other men walked behind.
Fox, Vixen and Dash watched their departure with
pounding hearts. Where would they go?

Fox told Vixen to stay with Dash. Then, keeping
well back, he followed the men, sinking to his belly
instantly when any one of the walkers turned his head.
In this way he trailed the men to the Warden's cottage.

Now Fox received a new shock. The Warden himself
opened the Park gate, a heavy wooden structure, to
allow the van to leave. Fox, hidden behind a tree stump
(a casualty of the storm), recognized the man who
for so long had been the Park's guardian. Here was
something he really couldn't comprehend. Why was

the Warden permitting wildlife to be captured and removed from his own preserve? The van trundled away down the drive. The Warden and the other men went inside the cottage, talking amongst themselves. Fox slunk away, sore at heart.

Dash and Vixen came to meet him. Fox described with bewilderment what he had seen. Dash, her thoughts constantly occupied with Plucky, reacted with the utmost vexation. 'Where did the humans go? Which way? Which way?' she shrilled.

'The Warden took them into his den,' Fox replied.

'But the machine, Fox, the machine!' Dash cried. She was frantic. 'The humans' machine with the animals inside! Where has it gone?'

Fox could see he had been lax in not keeping the van in view. 'I'm sorry, Dash. I couldn't follow it after it left the Park. It was too fast for – '

'I can follow it,' Dash broke in urgently. 'It can't be too fast for me.' She had so much confidence in her own speed she couldn't believe anything was faster. 'Now, show me which direction to take!'

Fox was alarmed and looked at Vixen with misgiving. 'You mustn't go racing after humans,' he warned emphatically. 'They're unpredictable and dangerous. Anything could happen.'

'*I'll* worry about that,' Dash answered bravely. 'Don't you see, I'm the only animal who has even a chance of discovering where our friends are being taken. And we're losing time now, precious time, Fox. Quickly, show me where to go, I beg you. It may be our last opportunity.'

Fox succumbed to her pleading and led her at a run to the Park gate. Luckily it was still open. Dash took his directions and galloped away in hot pursuit of the van. So swiftly did she bound along that she seemed like no more than a mere blur of speed. Fox and Vixen returned to cover with sinking spirits. Neither of them could imagine Dash would succeed in her mad undertaking, and they didn't expect ever to see her again.

Meanwhile Dash pounded along the track leading from the Park to the open road. She soon saw the van ahead. The vehicle had necessarily continued to travel slowly, loaded as it was with livestock. The fleet-footed young hare was able to gain on it, gradually reducing the distance. Eventually, however, the track ended and the van turned into the road and accelerated away. Dash sped to the end of the track. She saw the road and recoiled, nervous of its frightening aspect. There were other vehicles passing along the road and she knew there was no possibility of her pursuing the van on that route.

But she was loath to give up. A moment's consideration brought her attention to the fact that the downland overlooked this road, running parallel to it. She could run over the grass, therefore, and keep the road in view. Quick as lightning, she leapt from the track on to the springy turf. Then she raced away, keeping the road on her right all along. She had some ground to make up now, because the van was moving much faster. At last Dash had found her moment to test herself. Now she'd find out whether she actually was the champion runner she believed she was. Exerting all her strength, she urged herself forward faster and faster, glorying more than ever in the power of her young body. She streaked towards the horizon and, a few minutes later, she saw the object of her chase – the van – down below on the road. The vehicle had come to a halt and was preparing to turn into another track through the very countryside Dash herself was traversing. She brought her helter-skelter pace under control and, creeping carefully to a screen of blackthorn, watched where the van went.

'I didn't lose them, I didn't lose them,' she chattered to herself, thrilled to think that her speed alone had retained a link between her friends in the Park and those taken away from it. She saw the van go rocking over the uneven stony track and, when she felt it was far enough from her that she dared move again, she herself dropped down to the track and loped along in its wake.

After a short journey the van, with Dash well to its rear, began to approach a high wall which ran across their path at right angles. There was a double door in its centre. The driver of the van unlocked the doors and swung them wide open. The van then proceeded inside the walled area and, just before the gates were closed again, Dash had time to see on the other side of the wall a vista of greenery – pasture, clumps of trees and stretches of woodland very reminiscent of White Deer Park itself. There was nothing more for her to do now. She couldn't get inside this other enclosure, but she had the knowledge she had hoped for. She knew – and she could pass the information on to the others – exactly where the White Deer Park animals, Plucky and Weasel included, had been taken.

Excited as Dash was by her discovery, it didn't take her long to retrace her journey over the downland to the track leading to home. Here, her head full of the important news, she was not as alert to human activity as she should have been. As she approached the Park gate the Warden's Range Rover swung into the drive and Dash barely managed to skip aside to avoid it. The Warden himself and the other men who had been engaged in the roundup were aboard. Dash shot through the open gate and didn't stop running until she was well clear of the area. The gate was closed on the intrepid brown hare and she was safe once more within the boundaries of the Reserve. The Range Rover then continued its journey to the walled park in which the van, with its complement of animals, was now confined.

Dash hardly paused to draw breath before she plunged on to warn her friends. Fox and Vixen had returned to their home area, where Badger, Friendly and Leveret had joined them to learn the latest tidings. Even as Fox was describing Dash's courageous venture, the young hare tumbled into their midst, tired, excited and brimful of pride.

'Did – did you succeed?' Fox gasped, hardly able to believe his eyes.

'I did. And in every respect,' Dash answered a little boastfully. 'I followed the men the whole way and I've seen the place where all the creatures have been taken. It's like a – like a – well, another park, actually. I don't understand what this is all about. Are the animals to be released there? And if so, why was it necessary to remove them from here in the first place? There seems so little difference between the two.' She looked all around for a reaction but none of the others seemed to have any suggestions to offer. They looked, each one of them, completely nonplussed. Then suddenly they all started talking at once, demanding to know exactly what this second 'park' was like. Dash described what she had seen as best she could. Then she ended by saying,' 'There's one big difference from White Deer Park I should have told you about.'

'What's that?' Fox barked eagerly.

'There's no mere fence around the other place like there is here,' she answered importantly. 'It has a much more forbidding barrier – higher and stronger-looking. I can't imagine any creature could make a bid for freedom through that.'

'Not through it, Dash, naturally,' Leveret said. 'But why not over it, perhaps?'

'Far too high, Father,' said Dash categorically.

'Then maybe under it?'

Dash pondered. 'I don't think so,' she said slowly. 'It looks far too solid and there's no kind of gap anywhere like you see in places in the fence here.'

'It's banishment then,' Friendly summed up, 'for all those poor unfortunate beasts, even if they are released into the open. They're entirely in human hands.' He had voiced all their thoughts.

Fox looked fierce. 'We can't let this happen to Weasel,' he vowed. 'Or Plucky.' He looked all around. 'We're not going to let the humans tamper with our friends' lives like this, are we?'

'Of course not. We must help them,' Friendly responded resolutely.

'I'm always ready,' Badger began quaveringly, 'er – to do anything within my power.'

The others knew that power was severely limited. Badger's campaigning days were thought to be long over. 'My dear old friend,' Fox said warmly, 'your help and advice would be of the utmost value. What do you propose?'

'Propose? Why – to rescue them, of course. Rescue them. What else have we ever done when our friends have been in danger? Remember the Oath we all swore!' His old voice shook. 'That's what binds us together; whether in Farthing Wood or White Deer Park. The Oath of Mutual Protection means just that. There's no time to waste on this, we must act,' he finished rousingly.

'Dear Badger,' Vixen whispered.

'There must be a rescue party,' Badger went on. 'Fox, you're the organizer. You must arrange it. But you can count on me.'

'I know I can,' Fox said. But he looked sad. The idea of the aged animal accompanying such a party was out of the question. He sniffed at his old friend's grizzly fur and wagged his tail affectionately. 'You know, you'll be of most use here,' Fox told him. 'We need someone to keep tabs on those rats and there's simply no creature better qualified to take charge of that.'

'As you wish,' Badger replied. He was not too displeased with his appointment.

'So – to the rescue group,' Fox continued. 'Vixen and myself and Friendly will all go. Dash, you of course will be our guide. But we need, I think, a couple of good diggers. Would Mossy go?'

'Much too far for him to travel,' Dash answered at once. 'One of the rabbits would be a better bet. They can all run well enough.'

'No – no rabbits,' Fox said firmly. 'They're too unreliable.' He had never forgotten the panicky rabbits from Farthing Wood who had nearly cost him his life when crossing a river. 'Who else can dig?'

'Hedgehogs?' Friendly ventured.

'No, too slow across ground again,' Dash ruled.

'We'll have to discard the idea of digging then,' said Fox. 'What we really need is the help of the birds. One of us has to get inside the – er – compound to see the lie of the land and, more importantly, to locate the animals themselves. Whistler's out of the question at present.'

'That leaves Tawny Owl,' Friendly summarized neatly.

The friends exchanged glances. Every one of them appeared doubtful on that point.

'Will he co-operate?' Leveret asked finally.

'We can but ask,' said Fox. 'He's a strange old bird.

Holly seems to have taken him over, but if we appeal to his sense of loyalty, I think he'll respond.'

'Of course he'll respond,' Badger remarked. 'When has he ever been found wanting?'

'Badger, you always think the best of everyone,' said Fox. 'All credit to your stout old heart. But would Owl put himself out for Weasel's sake?'

'Hm. That could be a difficulty,' Badger admitted. 'They always struck sparks off each other. It needs a bit of diplomacy, this. I'll undertake to win him over. We're old companions and I think I know how to approach him.'

'I think you do, too,' Fox said wonderingly. 'My, you almost seem back to your old self. I've never seen you so determined since – since – '

'Since the old days?' Badger asked wryly with a twinkle in his eye. 'I think perhaps you're right, Fox. But you see, all I need is a sense of purpose.'

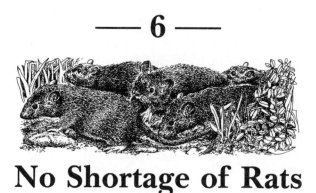

6

No Shortage of Rats

The friends were aware that the roundups were continuing. Animals in the Park talked of nothing else. There was widespread alarm. Fox racked his brains for a solution to the role of the Warden in all this. He simply couldn't understand the involvement of the man who was, or at any rate had been, regarded as their protector. He began to wonder if there was some benign purpose behind the transfer of various unlucky creatures to that other enclosure. Was it to give them a new start in a new home, perhaps? But why would they need that? He was unable to reach a conclusion. Then he thought hard about the rescue plan. The Farthing Wood animals had to get Weasel and Plucky back to the fold. None of them could accept that they must live in separate places. And then, supposing other creatures wanted to return to White Deer Park? They had all been uprooted from their homes and must be keen to get back to them. Fox's party would have to try and help them too. But how? How could they get them out?

Badger, true to his word, sought out Tawny Owl to induce him to be one of that party. He found him, in company with Holly, his mate, feeding from their night's tally of rats. Badger was delighted to see that

the owls were conscientiously playing their part in
keeping the rats' numbers down and he said as much.

'Hunting's never been easier,' Tawny Owl told him.
'One doesn't have to look far for prey these days.'

'The only danger is eating to excess,' Holly
remarked. 'The temptation to do so is certainly there.'

Tawny Owl gulped down another mouthful. 'We
have to eradicate this rat problem,' he said, as though
justifying himself. Holly glanced at Badger with a look
that said that in her view Owl was making full use of
the situation. Badger ignored this and said, 'Actually,
your help is needed in another way.'

Tawny Owl ruffled his feathers and resettled them.
'In what way?' he asked in an uninterested tone.

Badger explained how Dash had discovered the
walled enclosure and how only a bird could surmount
that wall.

'And that's to be me, is it?' Tawny Owl summed up.
'Of course, it would be,' he continued sarcastically,
'Just one more occasion for old Owl to stick his neck
out.'

'There'd really be no risk attached to it,' Badger
persuaded him.

'Oh no, of course not. Only that no-one knows
exactly what's behind this wall, I suppose, and I'm
naturally to be the one to find out?'

'Well, yes.'

'So if there are groups of humans standing around
shooting off guns, for instance, and then you don't see
me return, you'll all know that this new area is one to
be avoided, eh?'

'Oh really, Owl! Is that likely?' Badger exclaimed
irritably. 'Since when has the Warden gone around
taking pot-shots at his charges?'

'The Warden? What's he to do with it?' Owl asked
more quietly.

'We think he's organizing the transfer of the animals who have been captured.'

'Hm. That does put a different complexion on it, I imagine,' the bird said, somewhat mollified.

'Of course it does. And, I'm sure you'll agree, we have to find out where Weasel is and get him back.'

'Oh, so that's it? I'm to go searching for Weasel, am I? Oh, that's priceless, Badger. Me, of all creatures! The very bird he drove out of this Reserve with his taunts and gibes!'

'Now, Owl, you know that's an exaggeration and really, by now, the two of you should be reconciled.'

'They are,' Holly cut in. 'Owl knows that he owes Weasel a debt in part for finding *me*.'

'Of course, dear Holly, of course,' Tawny Owl hooted hastily. 'There were compensations.'

'Compensations!' cried Holly. 'Is that how you see me? A compensation?'

Tawny Owl was tying himself up in knots. 'I didn't mean that,' he floundered. 'You mistake me. You're the best thing that ever happened to me.' He didn't sound all that convincing and he looked helplessly at Badger.

'This is not achieving anything,' the old animal complained. He decided to use a blunter approach and really put Tawny Owl on the spot. 'Weasel needs your help. Are you prepared to give it?'

Tawny Owl could only give one answer to that. 'Oh, of course,' he muttered, 'if you put it that way . . .'

'Well?'

'Naturally I'll do all I can.' Tawny Owl shifted his stance, glancing surreptitiously at Holly to gauge her reaction.

'You told me there'd be no more adventuring,' she reminded him curtly.

'It's not actually an adventure, you see, Holly,' the old bird excused himself. 'Is it, Badger?'

'No. It's a rescue,' Badger explained. 'And there is not only Weasel to think about. Plucky is still missing too.'

'Well, he'll have to go, whether he wishes to or not,' Holly said. 'I know all about your precious Oath.'

'Good,' Badger said with satisfaction. 'Then it's settled. There's no-one as skilful or as accurate as Tawny Owl in the dark.'

Owl preened himself. 'When do we go?' he asked.

'Soon. Fox will decide when the time is right. I myself won't be one of the group, which I regret. However, there are things to be done here too.'

Badger's words were prophetic. Under cover of night more rats were arriving in the Park and claiming it for their home. During daylight hours they kept out of sight, escaping human observation. So, amongst the animals being rounded up for transfer, were some of the very predators who could have kept the rats in check. The infiltrators were able to use this easy situation to colonize areas of the Park. They were free to establish their nests and runs near the stream and close to the Pond. They liked to be close to water, and Toad and the Edible Frogs watched the rats' swelling numbers with the greatest alarm. Toad knew that at the very time when the hunters of the Reserve were needed more than ever, there were fewer of them around.

Of course the rats suffered losses, but their adaptability to all kinds of conditions, their purposefulness and cunning enabled them to recover from any setbacks. They ate anything that came their way: carrion, seeds, berries, fungi, small animals such as mice, insects and worms. They sometimes raided birds' nests for eggs and fledglings. They were savage and eager killers, and many parent birds deserted their nests or saw them ravaged. The rats were excellent climbers and swimmers. There was not one area of the Park where they didn't leave their mark. And with each day that passed, more of them arrived, having heard about the perfect refuge away from the molestation of Man and his traps and poisons.

The Farthing Wood animals did their level best to combat the threat, as did many another creature born and reared in the Reserve. Tawny Owl and Holly continued to pounce on the rats running at night over the leaf litter on the wood bottom. The foxes accounted for more. But Weasel, who was a fearsome ratter, was sorely missed, and the animals made no more than a small dent in the rats' numbers. The invasion could not be held back.

The resident animals in the Park began to find that their usual food was becoming short. They could foresee that, if the present trend should continue, starvation might soon be staring them in the face.

'We need to get the other predator animals back here to turn the tide,' Badger insisted to Fox. 'Why do you delay? The whole of the Park will be swamped!'

'I've been waiting for a move from the Warden,' Fox defended himself. 'But it seems he's no longer our protector. How *can* he be blind to what's occurring here?'

'We can't wait for human intervention in this case,' Badger told him. 'The men are concentrating their attention on the new Reserve.'

Fox looked at Badger sharply. 'What's that you say? A new Reserve?'

'Yes, yes, the other enclosure,' Badger grunted. 'What else can it be? Those animals that have been rounded up and caught must have been moved to build up a stock in a new Reserve. The Warden has turned his back on White Deer Park in favour of the new place. Dash told us it looked very similar. Perhaps the creatures we thought were unfortunate are the *fortunate* ones because they've been moved away from the menace of the rats.'

'And us: we're to be left in the lurch?' Fox muttered bitterly. 'It doesn't make sense, Badger. This has always been a nature reserve. Why abandon it to an army of rats? And what about the deer? They're the Warden's prime responsibility.'

'Will they be moved too, eventually?' Badger whispered. He hardly dared give voice to his thoughts, for, with the deer elsewhere, there would no longer be a White Deer Park as they had always known it, and then its special status would disappear.

'That's too awful to contemplate,' Fox said hoarsely. 'We must prevent *their* removal, at all costs. And the way to do that is to wage war against the rats. We need every tooth and claw, every beak and talon on our side. Our first task, therefore, is to construct an entry point into the new enclosure; then we can set about gathering support.' He looked directly at Badger. 'Old friend,' he said, 'I'm leaving you in charge here. These are critical times for White Deer Park. Dash must lead us to the other Reserve tonight. You were quite right. We can't afford to wait a moment longer.'

7

The New Park

It was a cloudy night and as dark as the little group of would-be rescuers could hope for. The Park gate of course being closed, Dash, Fox, Vixen and Friendly made their way silently to Dash's scrape under the boundary fence. One by one they squeezed underneath while Tawny Owl perched on the fence top. 'All through?' he hooted.

'All through,' Fox confirmed. 'Now, Dash, lead on. Go swiftly, but don't lose us.'

The young hare, tingling with self-importance, ran ahead. Tawny Owl kept up with her, flying directly above. The foxes, led by Friendly, who was the youngest of them, brought up the rear. They pattered silently alongside the fence, following its curve until they reached the track leading from the Park gate. Now Dash's long hind legs began to kick faster. She glanced behind to make sure the foxes were keeping up. 'We're with you,' Friendly assured her. Dash accelerated towards the road.

'Where are you going?' Tawny Owl called down. 'You're heading for trouble that way.'

Dash ignored him, safe in the knowledge that she had travelled the route before. The bird continued to protest; then Dash leapt away at the last moment, leaving the track and bounding across the downland adjacent to the road. 'I know the way, old Owl, I know the way,' she whispered. Tawny Owl caught by surprise at her sudden change of direction and pace, banked sharply to follow the hare, and almost collided with a road sign. Muttering imprecations at the folly and conceit of youngsters, he beat his wings hastily to keep abreast of the animals.

In a little while the five of them were outside the walls of the other enclosure. 'Anything behind those is well and truly sealed in,' Friendly commented.

'Owl, you're our only hope now,' Fox told his old companion as the bird alighted on the top of the wall. 'See what you can discover: whether there is the slightest chink in this formidable barrier.'

Tawny Owl's head swivelled round a hundred and eighty degrees as he scanned the murky spaces of the strange park. His huge eyes blinked in the blanket of the night and he made preparatory flaps of his wings.

'Do I – um – call for Weasel?' he asked diffidently.

'Yes. Try to find him; his knowledge of this place will be of value. However little he knows about it, it will be more than we do.'

'All right, Fox. I suppose he'll recognize my cry,' Tawny Owl said, and he launched himself from the wall.

'I wish you'd told him to keep a lookout for Plucky,' Dash said regretfully.

'Weasel's sure to know if Plucky is around,' Vixen said, trying to comfort her.

'All will be well.'

Tawny Owl swooped over the unfamiliar parkland, calling intermittently. He soon discovered this enclosure was far smaller than White Deer Park, although its terrain was broadly similar. Indeed the comparison with the Nature Reserve was sufficiently striking for

Owl to begin to wonder if he wasn't flying over its companion park.

'It makes sense,' he told himself, 'if our Reserve is overcrowded to move some of the overflow, as it were, to another place where life can be lived just the same.' He was very pleased with his deduction and thought how much cleverer he was than Fox or anyone else to have arrived at this conclusion. 'Of course,' he mused, 'the trouble is, whereas the animals have been moved, their nests haven't. Which means they have to start all over again.'

After flying over much of the enclosure, quartering the area as thoroughly as he could, Owl became a little impatient. He started to call more regularly and more loudly. 'Weasel! Weasel! Can you hear me? It's Owl!' Then he broke off to complain to himself. ('He knows I'm here, how can he not answer? He's avoiding me; it's a deliberate ploy. Oh, what sort of a creature is he? This is no game. Weasel! Weasel! (Calls himself a friend! A fine friend, putting me to all this trouble and effort.) WEASEL!!'

The owl perched in a pine tree to rest for a while. Below him was the widest spread of woodland he had found in the enclosure. 'If he's not hiding himself some-where in there, then I'm a kingfisher,' he declared. 'Ideal spot, just like Farthing Wood used to be. I'll wait around and *he* can come to *me*, if he deigns to make contact. I've done all I can to find *him*.'

His occasional irritable cries: 'Ke-wick! Ke-wick!' instantly recognizable by all his old companions as the owl's personal hallmark brought not Weasel but Plucky running towards the sound.

'Owl? Is it you?' the young fox barked excitedly. 'Ah – I see you. *How* you've been calling!'

'Oh, Plucky.' Owl acknowledged the young fox with some relief and not without pleasure. 'I've flown up and down this place in all directions. I thought I'd never rouse anybody. It's good to know *you're* not deaf!'

'Far from it. What are you doing here?'

'Well – looking for you, obviously,' Tawny Owl replied testily. 'And, as you have no doubt gathered, Weasel too.'

'I'm not surprised you haven't found Weasel,' Plucky said. 'He's part of the tunnelling party. He's probably underground even now and so he couldn't have picked up your call.'

'Underground? Typical!' Tawny Owl rasped. 'What's the good of being underground when I've been wearing my wings out in search of him?'

'Excuse my saying so,' said Plucky politely, 'but how was Weasel to know you'd come looking for him?'

'Well, well, never mind that now,' Tawny Owl responded. 'I'm glad to see *you* anyway, young fellow. Fox, Vixen and Friendly have come on a mission of rescue. And,' he added slyly, 'there's another interested party alongside them who can't wait to know if you're safe.'

Plucky guessed at once who he meant. 'Dash?' he cried. 'She's not lost then?'

'Of course she's not lost. She discovered this place, actually. And Plucky, tell me, what is it? Is it a park? What do you do here?'

'Do here? Well, try to think of ways of getting out, principally. And that's what Weasel's engaged on with the others. But – yes, I suppose it is a sort of park. Everything goes on just like in White Deer Park. Once we were released by the men, we were left alone to live as we did before. I think some of the animals have quite settled down. They have all they want. Others, though, want to get back to their real homes. Some of them have been parted from their families. It's all so strange – I don't know why we were suddenly uprooted in this way.'

'I have a theory about that,' Tawny Owl told him. 'But we'll leave that for later. Have you reconnoitred the whole area? Because the important thing is whether there is a way out: a gap in the wall or – or – anything like that.'

'Nothing,' Plucky answered definitively. 'Not the tiniest crack. This place cannot be breached, not even by the smallest mouse, unless he or she's a champion climber. I don't think anything except a bird like yourself can get in or out without human sanction.'

'What about this tunnelling business you said Weasel's involved in? Have there been any successes?'

'None that I know of. A number of animals like Weasel – stoats, hedgehogs and a young badger – have been trying to dig down below the wall at different points. But it seems the construction goes down so deep they haven't managed so far to get underneath it. There are no moles around – of course the humans couldn't round any of *them* up. And I believe only a posse of moles could dig the sort of tunnel that's needed here.'

'Do you know where Weasel is? Can you find him?' Owl requested. 'He may have some new information.'

'I doubt that,' Plucky said. 'But yes, I'll fetch him at once. I know what stretch of the wall they're digging by. Will you wait here?'

'Yes, I've tired myself out for the present. Will you be quick?'

'As quick as a fox can run.'

As Plucky vanished, Tawny Owl derived some satisfaction from the knowledge that Weasel was obliged to come all the way from the enclosure wall to where he was now perching comfortably on a branch of the Scots pine. It was as though the beast had to do the bird's bidding and, if Owl had been capable of it, he would have hugged himself.

Weasel came willingly enough. He couldn't quite reconcile himself to the idea of Tawny Owl posing as his saviour, but he was keen to find out the truth. Owl stretched his wings and adopted a majestic stance as he saw Weasel and Plucky approaching. But Weasel soon took the wind out of his sails.

'Well, I *am* honoured,' he quipped, 'that you should fly all this way for my benefit!'

'I didn't,' Tawny Owl corrected him irritably. 'Don't flatter yourself, Weasel. Fox put me in the position of being unable to refuse.'

'Refuse what?'

'To join the rescue party, of course.'

'What rescue party? Where are the others?' Weasel asked.

'They're waiting for me, outside this – this – park or whatever it is. I was sent in to discover a – um – loophole. I'm told by Plucky there isn't one, unless you've discovered something?'

'I'll tell you what I've discovered,' Weasel offered. 'And that is, that there's no way out of here for a creature on four legs. We've dug and dug, the other digging animals and I, and the wall goes down and down and at the bottom there's something so thick and incomparably hard that it might as well be solid rock. So, like it or not, we're here to stay. As far as a rescue party goes, the only way for them to get inside here is to get themselves captured like I did!'

'Just how would that help?' Owl returned scathingly.

'It wouldn't. I'm not suggesting anyone adopts the idea, you foolish feathered – '

'Don't you take out your frustrations on me,' Owl interrupted angrily. 'You shouldn't have allowed yourself to get into human hands in the first place!'

'Oh, let me cut through all this,' Plucky pleaded. 'We're supposed to be helping each other, aren't we? Owl, can't you at least go and tell Fox and – um – the others, you know – that you've found us and we're quite safe?'

'Of course I can, and I'll do so at once,' the bird agreed. He looked down at Weasel with just a hint of sympathy. 'It doesn't do any good to fall out,' he remarked. 'I – er – I'm sorry, Weasel, for your predicament. I'm sure you never asked to be brought here.'

Weasel was mollified. 'No, indeed I didn't. And I thank you for expressing yourself in that way. We haven't always got on, I know, but you're not really a bad old bird.'

'I'm glad you think so,' Owl found himself saying. 'I'll delay no longer then. We'll try to think of another plan and, in the meantime, you must take care of yourselves, both of you.'

'Holly must have softened him,' Weasel observed as he watched Tawny Owl glide away. 'He never used to talk in those tones.'

Dash and the foxes were in a fever of impatience. Tawny Owl seemed to them to have been gone for ages. At last they saw his silent shadowy form swoop over the wall. The bird landed at their feet.

'It's no use,' he announced, and hastily explained why. He described the terrain of the enclosure and finished by saying, 'Along with the other animals here, Weasel and Plucky are safe, and they're also just about as secure as human ingenuity can devise.'

8

Airlift

There was no choice for the frustrated rescue party but to return to White Deer Park. They reached Dash's scrape without mishap, but each of them was disappointed with the night's outcome. Dash felt immensely relieved now that she knew for certain where Plucky was. She wondered if she and the young fox would ever be able to run and play together again, and spoke her doubts out loud. Fox looked determined. 'I confess I'm temporarily beaten,' he said, 'but this isn't the end of the matter. I'm going to get Weasel and Plucky out of there one way or another. The others will have to take their chances – I can't be responsible for everyone. But the Farthing Wood community is incomplete and I do have a duty to put that right.'

'Not you alone,' Vixen reminded him. 'We all have a part to play, don't we Owl?'

'Yes, of course, Vixen,' the bird hooted agreeably, although he was actually of the opinion that he had done all he could and hoped not to be troubled again. Holly was brooding her eggs and he was aware that feeding their nestlings would be a full-time occupation, so he tried to cover himself against any future activities. 'You know, that enclosure is not so very awful. Plucky admitted to me that the animals in it can live just as they do here. I've come to believe the humans had their best interests in mind when they moved them there.'

'So you think it's another nature reserve too?' Fox asked. 'Badger thinks as much and it *is* the most plausible explanation.'

'As a matter of fact,' Tawny Owl ventured to say, 'there are benefits for all of us in this development. We all have more space.'

'You've forgotten something,' Friendly said. 'More space for us means more scope for the rats to fill the gaps.'

The rat problem wouldn't go away. Although their numbers appeared to have stabilized the residents of White Deer Park couldn't feel comfortable in their own home. Each of them regarded the rats as aliens. The rats were known to be prolific breeders and the other animals feared a population explosion. Try as they did, the hunters of the Park couldn't seem to make any real inroads into the rat colonies. As fast as they caught them, others took their place. 'There are too many of them and not enough of us,' was Badger's comment. 'We need Weasel badly, and as many of his kind as we can get.'

However, the rats couldn't escape human notice for ever. In fact it was only because the Warden's interest had been absorbed elsewhere that they had prospered at all. Naturally, in the long run, some of them were bound to fall foul of the beaters and the line of nets. These, flushed from their nests, scuttled into the obstacle and at once focused the attention of their captors. The animals at last had allies, and powerful ones too.

The rats needed all their cunning, and this was impressive indeed. They were long used to the schemes and tactics of humans and had their own ways of com-

batting them. Once some of their number had fallen
victim to the nets, they knew the humans' next move
would be to seek out their nests and burrows and
attempt to exterminate them. So word had passed from
one colony to another to move beyond their reach. The
older rats knew White Deer Park was a nature reserve.
That was why they had led the migration there. Their
chief concern in life was to evade their human foes,
who harried them everywhere. Now it seemed clear
that humans had pursued them even to this haven.
They knew nothing about the men's real purpose, nor
anything of the existence of the other park. But they
did know always that they had to keep one step ahead.

Under cover of night the bulk of the adult rats began
to traverse the Park, moving from the runs and burrows
of their new settlements and returning to the dank,
warm and odorous channels and ditches of the local
sewer system. They loved the safety of these tunnels in
the winter months. They were able to keep snug and
well fed. In the summer they preferred the countryside
but, for the present, the countryside they had chosen
was fraught with danger. When danger threatened
them, the rats always responded. Only nursing females
were left behind in the Nature Reserve, and then only
from necessity. When the time was right and the Park
was peaceful again, the sewer rats would rejoin them
and breathe country air once more.

One of the biggest males, a rat called Bully, vowed
revenge on the animals who had hunted them there
and egged his companions on to do the same. 'We can't
fight two enemies,' he growled. 'A retreat was essential
– temporarily. When the humans think they've driven
us out they'll relax their guard. They'll have other
plans to put into operation: they have so many buzzing
in their great heads, don't they? Then we rats will be
overlooked and we can steal back, just a bunch of us

at a time, and build up our colonies again. Eventually we'll be more than a match for any beast or bird who wants to take us on. If you listen to me, all of you, and do as I say, we can take over the entire Reserve – yes, even from the deer. We'll be so numerous we'll – we'll *flood* them into submission. Are you with old Bully or against him?'

The other rats chorused their support and approval just as he knew they would. He was a natural leader and they needed a strong voice to give them direction.

'So be it,' he grunted. 'We'll bide our time here in the old familiar network with its rich ripe scents. *We* don't mind, do we? We *like* strong smells; the stronger the better. They make us feel at home. But we can also have a change when we feel like it, can't we? And when we do, we'll go, and next time *nothing* will stop us.'

The astonishing abruptness of the rats' drop in numbers was very encouraging to the Farthing Wood animals. They attributed it to human action and they weren't far wrong. Now they had more time to concentrate on devising a new plan to bring Weasel and Plucky back into the fold. Fox thought he might have the remedy for restoring Weasel to where he belonged, though Plucky would be more of a problem. He went to see how Whistler was faring.

The heron was easy to find. He stood on the stream's bank in his habitually rigid and motionless stance. He stared down at the water as if lost in contemplation of whether there was edible life in it or not.

'Glad to see you, Whistler,' Fox greeted him warmly. 'How's the fishing?'

Whistler's absorption was broken. He stepped back. 'I'm glad to see you too,' he said in his slow voice. 'The fishing is – how shall I put it? – debatable.'

'Do you catch anything these days?'

'Rarely. I took a fish yesterday. I almost regretted it afterwards; it seemed a lonely thing, swimming around by itself. I don't want to deplete the fish stock just as it's been introduced to the stream again. I feel I should wait until they've multiplied somewhat but, then again, how can I? I have to eat.'

'I can see you've lost weight,' Fox remarked sympathetically. 'Is there nowhere else you can fly to?'

'There is, but flying's painful just now. I'm up against it, Fox. Worms, slugs and snails form the basis of my diet. I sometimes wonder what's happening to my insides.'

'Are you able to fly short distances?' Fox asked. 'There's going to be a glut of young frogs in the pond, by all accounts; too many for their own good. Could you make use of that?'

'I suppose I could. Of course they won't be of any great size for a long while. Just morsels, you see, for me. I'm desperate to get a substantial meal into my bill. And then, I feel awkward about the Pond. I don't like to think I'd be poaching Toad's friends and relatives under his very nose.'

'It wouldn't concern him, I can assure you, Whistler. I tell you – there are too many of them. Toad said so himself. But, look, I must come to the point. I'm here to put a proposition to you.'

'I see. Speak on, Fox.'

'We know where Weasel is.' Fox described how Tawny Owl had found him and how Weasel was trapped in the enclosure, along with Plucky and others. 'Weasel's a small creature,' Fox went on carefully. 'Do you remember, on our journey to White Deer Park, how we all crossed the motorway?'

'Certainly I do,' Whistler verified. 'Vividly. I remember exactly how – oh, now I understand!' he interrupted himself, with some amusement. 'You're thinking of how I carried Weasel across the road.'

'Exactly. You carried him then. Could you do so again? Just over the Park wall and no further?'

'Hm. I'm a bit creaky, to tell you the truth. I'd be more than willing to try, although I'd hate to drop him.'

'I'm sure you wouldn't do that. He's awfully slight, isn't he? Perhaps you could practise first with a stick or two?'

'Indeed I will,' said the heron. 'But I need to build my strength up.'

'All right,' said Fox. 'I'll catch you some rats.'

Rat-catching had become a way of life in White Deer Park. Suddenly there were very few rats around. The animals hardly dared hope they had the invaders licked. Fox and Vixen pounced on the odd female rat out scavenging for her young and ferried their prey to Whistler, who dispatched it with great relish. 'I'm most grateful,' he told them. 'If the rats would only show themselves in daylight, I could go hunting myself.'

The heron felt heartened by the improvement in his nutrition. He began to search for stout pieces of wood. One day, while juggling with various twigs and sticks in a meditative sort of way, he was surprised by Adder, who slid into view unexpectedly.

'Whatever are you doing?' the snake hissed. 'You're not thinking of swallowing those, are you?'

'Oh, Adder! I thought I was alone,' Whistler said, feeling a little foolish. 'No, it's all part of my exercise scheme. I have an important task to accomplish.'

'And what is that? Building a new kind of nest?'

The heron croaked raucously. 'Krornk!' he was much amused. 'You're a wry one, Adder. I'm too ancient to pair. No female would be interested in an arthritic old has-been like me. No, I'm going to airlift Weasel.'

Adder leered. 'What a novel idea.'

'Not so novel,' Whistler corrected him. 'Remember the motorway? I seem to recall you also found yourself whisked off on that day.'

Adder did remember and he hastily coiled himself around a fallen branch in case Whistler intended to repeat the trick by way of a test.

Whistler put his head on one side and stepped close. 'Are you game for a little practice?' He was joking but Adder took him seriously. The snake shot from the branch and wriggled with the utmost swiftness towards the stream, where he plunged straight in. The last Whistler saw of him, Adder was rapidly looping his way downstream with only his head above water, as if expecting the heron's long bill to snatch him up at any moment.

The whole episode put Whistler in much lighter spirits than he had enjoyed for a long time. He felt ready to tackle his mission of rescue. He beat his old wings once or twice with gritty determination, trying to ignore his aches and pains. Then he took off for Fox's earth.

Fox had already primed Tawny Owl to be available to show Whistler the way when the time was right. Owl had grumbled, telling Fox about Holly's three white eggs, which were due to hatch any moment, but the bird had seen no real alternative to falling in with the plan. Consequently when Whistler arrived, Fox, having first welcomed the heron as a hero, referred him to Owl's roost in a hollow oak.

Whistler discovered Holly on her eggs. Tawny Owl was absent. 'He's asleep somewhere,' she told him. 'Can't you wait until evening?'

'I could wait until dusk,' the heron offered. 'I'm not too adept at nocturnal flights.'

'Well, the two of you must come to an arrangement. You can see I'm busy,' Holly told him tartly. 'You'll probably find him snoozing in one of the largest beeches. They remind him of his old home.'

Whistler was only too glad to leave. He felt out of place in the presence of brooding hen birds, now that his own mating days were over. He flew to the clump of mature beeches and circled awkwardly above them, keeping his eyes peeled for the sleepy owl. But the beeches' newly opened leaves screened Tawny Owl from view. He was well hidden, which was what he liked. Whistler called to him with his harsh croaky cry. It was a very loud cry. One or two repetitions woke Tawny Owl from his nap, as well as a number of other unlucky creatures who preferred to sleep by day.

'Is that you, Whistler?' Owl demanded. 'You might have allowed me a little more shut-eye! We're not all used to gallivanting around in the daytime.'

'I can wait,' Whistler replied amicably. 'I merely wanted to be sure you were in there. Ah – I can see you now. I'll perch here' – he alighted clumsily on a topmost bough – 'while you doze off again for a bit.'

'How can I doze off again now I'm awake?' Tawny Owl snapped. 'I can't turn sleep on and off like a – like a – '

'Like a cat?' Whistler suggested helpfully.

'Like whatever you please!' Tawny Owl retorted.

'I'm sorry to have disturbed you, really I am,' the heron apologized. 'It will soon be dusk. Shall we go then?'

'No point in waiting now, is there?' Tawny Owl mumbled. 'The sooner I've taken you to the spot, the sooner I can get back.'

'Just as you wish,' said Whistler.

Tawny Owl shuffled on to a branch, blinking sleepily. He stretched his wings and glared up at the heron.

The setting sun dazzled him and he closed his eyes tight. Whistler waited patiently until Owl was quite ready. Abruptly Tawny Owl leapt from the branch, flapping his silent wings and sailing upwards. He skimmed the tree-tops, just clipping Whistler's pate with one dangling toe as the heron prepared to follow him. The owl felt better after that, as though he had evened the score.

The two large birds soared over the Park, silhouetted against the sunset. Tawny Owl flew on a direct course to the new Reserve and landed on top of the wall. Whistler perched beside him.

'This is the place,' Tawny Owl said. 'You'll find Weasel soon enough if you call him.' His job done, the owl began at once his return journey, but the heron called him back. 'Wait! Wait, old friend!' Whistler cried.

Tawny Owl veered and landed again. 'Now what?' he demanded.

'Well, that's a large area in there,' the heron said. 'Can't you give me some clue as to where Weasel's likely to be?'

'Not really,' his guide answered unhelpfully. 'I had to find him the hard way – by calling and calling until he came.'

'But surely you must remember roughly where Weasel was when you found him?'

Tawny Owl pondered. It had been Plucky who had found Weasel, not he himself. 'No, Whistler, I can't,' he replied truthfully.

'Come now, I know I woke you up before you wished it, but why be so unhelpful?' the heron appealed to him. 'The thing is, Owl, my wings do give me discomfort if I fly too far. Be a good chap and save me combing the entire expanse, please.'

Tawny Owl relented. 'I'm sorry,' he said. 'You see,

Plucky came to my call, rather than Weasel. Of course you mustn't tax yourself. I'll try to direct you. I'll fly into the enclosure, and I may be able to pinpoint the spot where Plucky found me. You follow me.'

'I'm most awfully grateful,' the heron said with relief, and did just as Tawny Owl bade him.

Owl flew unerringly to the selfsame pine tree where he had halted in his search before. The two birds alighted and sat side by side. 'Now,' said Tawny Owl, 'call Plucky as well as Weasel. Then you're bound to find one of them.'

'I can't carry Plucky out of here,' Whistler protested, but his companion was already in the air, this time determined to return home.

'There's really no more I can do now,' Owl called over his spread wings.

Whistler settled himself more comfortably amongst the pine needles and, in the gathering dusk, called Weasel's name. 'I'd better not encourage Plucky,' he told himself, 'or he may expect too much of me.' His wing muscles ceased to ache and the heron resigned himself to a long wait. But, just as before, the alert Plucky recognized one of the familiar sounds of White Deer Park and tracked it down.

Whistler explained why he was there, emphasizing that he was only capable of carrying the smallest and lightest of animals. Plucky ran off to look for Weasel and to repeat the heron's message. He was excited at the prospect of Weasel being transported out of the enclosure by a bird. It seemed like playing the men at their own game. He found Weasel, wakeful in the spring evening, emerging from his makeshift nest. Plucky babbled out what Whistler had told him.

'Well!' Weasel exclaimed. 'I didn't expect this. I bet Fox is behind it, the clever old fellow.' He well remembered hanging limp in the heron's bill as he was whisked across the motorway all those seasons ago. 'Lead on, Plucky. This is a marvellous piece of news.'

Whistler fluttered to the ground as he saw them approaching. 'Here's your escape route, Weasel,' he quipped in his slow deep voice.

'Not for the first time,' Weasel answered appreciatively. 'I've been itching to get out of here. I'm really obliged to you, Whistler, because the tunnelling lark didn't work, and I saw myself separated from my friends for good.'

Plucky looked glum, as if reminded of his own position, and Whistler noticed it. 'I am so sorry,' he said to the fox, 'I can't extend my assistance to you too but, as you will appreciate . . .' He broke off. There was no need to say more.

'Don't let it worry you,' Plucky answered with feigned optimism. 'I'll get myself out, even if it means going out the same way I came in.'

Weasel and Whistler looked at him with puzzled expressions but Plucky wouldn't explain. He said quietly, 'Good luck, Weasel. And tell Dash when you see her we'll soon be running together again through our Park.'

Whistler cocked his head on one side. 'Are you ready then?' he asked.

Weasel said that he was. Whistler opened his beak and, very gently, grasped his friend until he had him in a firm grip. Then he took to the air, pleasantly surprised by Weasel's modest weight. Over the enclosure wall they went and then down on to the springy turf of the downland, where the heron released his passenger.

'Any discomfort?' Whistler asked.

'None at all,' Weasel assured him. 'Whistler, I'm in your debt.'

'Nonsense,' said the bird. 'You know the way now?'

'I should think I do,' said Weasel.

9

The Rats Gain Ground

Not long after Weasel's return he was able to find Dash and convey Plucky's words to her.

'I don't know what he means,' the hare said sadly. 'How can we ever be together again? He's not lucky enough to be small and he can never be carried back to his old home.'

Weasel began to feel a little guilty that he had left Plucky behind. 'I think he has a plan of his own,' he told Dash. 'He's quite determined to get back.'

Dash wasn't comforted. 'No,' she said. 'It's not possible. I shan't see him again. Even Fox can't compete with the humans' cleverness.'

'Well, he got me out,' Weasel reminded her and then immediately wished he hadn't. 'I mean to say, he's still trying to find a way to help Plucky.' He left Dash as soon as he decently could.

The hare moped about. These days she hardly ever felt like racing. As she nibbled listlessly at some bark she thought how lonely Plucky must be feeling with none of his friends around him. She wished fervently there was something she could do about it. All at once the idea come to her that there was something she *could* do about making him less lonely. She could join him! If Plucky couldn't come to her, she could go to him. She only had to find where the men were setting up their nets that day and then run headlong into them. She'd let the humans bring them together.

'Oh, why didn't I think of this before?' she berated herself. 'There's no fun in White Deer Park any more. I may as well go to the other place.' Now she did have a reason for running again. She had to locate the group of men before she could allow herself to be captured. She set off at once for the area where she had seen them operating before. Finding no human evidence there, she ran towards the Warden's cottage to see if they were gathering nearby for their day's work. All was quiet in the vicinity. There was no sign of any activity. Dash ran around the Park, searching systematically for the men she wanted to trap her. By the time she had covered the entire terrain of the Nature Reserve, she knew the men had gone. It seemed they had taken all the animals they needed and that their programme of capture and removal was over, at any rate for the time being. Dash sank down in some long grass close to where a number of the white deer were feeding. She felt tired and utterly deflated. The placid movements of the deer soothed and refreshed her after her exertions and she fell asleep in the sun.

The Farthing Wood animals had, between them, come close to piecing together what the actions of the Warden and his assistants had all been about. White Deer Park had been overpopulated. There was another piece of land nearby set aside exclusively for wildlife. So this had been used to take up the overspill. The fact that families had been split up, pairs separated, had not been the intention of the men, but this had been unavoidable in their efforts to ease the pressures on the Nature Reserve. The new enclosure had once been the walled grounds of a country house. The house had long ago fallen into disuse and disrepair. The land, meanwhile, had been bequeathed to the County Naturalists' Trust and so had fallen eventually under the White Deer Park Warden's jurisdiction. As yet the new reserve had no name. There were no deer in it and the Warden was still in discussions with another local landowner for further extending it.

As for White Deer Park itself, although it now returned to its usual aspect of a wildlife haven, tranquil and without human activity, it was actually under greater threat. This was because the rats saw the time was right for their return. The ruse had worked. The humans had been bamboozled by the rodents' temporary evacuation. After three rats had been discovered in the nets, no more had been found anywhere and the men had looked upon their capture, therefore, as isolated incidents. It had been easy for the sly creatures to congregate in the sewer system that they understood so well, and simply to wait until the alarm blew over. They kept tabs on the humans' doings in the Park by sending out an animal here and there to reconnoitre. Eventually news got back that the human presence had been withdrawn.

'Our patience has paid off,' said Bully to his comrades. 'The country air beckons again. We'll take that country air, shall we? *And* all the other benefits that go with it. The best of it is, the Park is unguarded now. But we won't be foolish or impulsive. We know better than that. A few at a time is the way to do it. We don't want to arouse suspicion. We can spread ourselves across the Park in stages. No-one's going to notice us. We're only small creatures, aren't we?'

The rats made their way back in tight little groups, over a period of many nights. They were so quiet and careful about it that the Park residents were unaware there was anything amiss, especially since they had ceased to keep a lookout recently because of the dearth of rodents. So when Dash opened her eyes in the early evening and saw, not deer, but a pair of rats scurrying through the grass, she thought nothing of it. Plucky was still uppermost in her mind.

Other animals around the Reserve spied rats separately in twos and threes. The true picture of the rats' planned invasion escaped them for some time. Whistler, who had acquired a taste for rats, caught one drinking from the stream. He looked for others along the stream's banks but found none. The thought occurred to him that he might spy some more by the Pond. And he did. He was able to spear another two, after which he stood on one leg and dozed.

The Pond became a favourite patrol area for Whistler. He ignored the young frogs and toads who were developing fast in the sun-warmed water, and kept his sharp eyes skinned for larger prey. And it was in this way, more than any other, that the rats' increasing numbers were first noticed. Whistler passed the news to Tawny Owl. He thought the other bird could profit from it, particularly with the prospect of young to feed.

'I'm grateful to you,' Owl acknowledged. 'The eggs have hatched and Holly and I have been kept busy. I've done the lion's share of fetching and carrying.'

'I thought you looked a bit ragged,' Whistler remarked jocularly.

Tawny Owl didn't take exception to this. 'I feel worn and weary,' he admitted. 'Parenthood's all very well but it's come to me a little late in life.'

'Better late than never, surely?'

'I don't know,' Owl answered. 'It's such a job finding sufficient prey. The owlets are always hungry. I've no sooner torn one meal to shreds for them than they're clamouring for more. And Holly keeps urging me to bring bigger quantities. I sometimes wonder if I'm appreciated at all.'

'Oh, the typical parent!' quipped Whistler. 'I know just how you feel, though. I bet you feel you never have time to grab a morsel yourself.'

'You've summed it up perfectly,' Tawny Owl grumbled. 'Holly says everything I catch I must bring to the nest. But I have to keep myself alive as well.'

'You'll get by,' Whistler chuckled. 'Snatch a bite here and there as you feed the young'uns. You can catch up again later when they're asleep.'

'I don't think they *ever* sleep,' Owl moaned.

'Well, the rats will be handy for you. They drink a lot at the Pond. Easy for an old campaigner like you to pick them off. How many nestlings do you have?'

'Three.'

'How charming. Are they sturdy?'

'Two of them are. One's lagging behind – the last one to hatch.'

'Hm. Well, if two out of three make it, you won't have done badly.'

'I suppose not,' Tawny Owl muttered.

'Anyway – the rats are back. So that's good news for all three of them.' It wasn't good news for anyone, of course. It was the worst possible news. The rats grabbed territory wherever they chose, pushing out mice and voles on land and any other creatures smaller than they were. They competed for space along the stream where water voles were just beginning to return now that there was healthy vegetation sprouting in its waters. The water voles were few and offered little resistance. By the Pond Toad watched the rats encroaching on the Edible Frogs' area and looking as if they would overwhelm the creatures' ancestral home.

The other Farthing Wood animals – Fox and Vixen, Badger and now, once more, Weasel – noticed disturbing signs of the rats' determination to populate every nook and cranny around the Park. The momentum of the rodents' advance was such that, within a matter of a few weeks, only the central portions of the Reserve remained free of them; and this was because they were mostly grassland and access to water was less easy. To all the residents there seemed to be several times as many rats as there ever had been. They were alarmed at the way they were losing ground to the invaders right across the Reserve. The more timid animals ran before the rats and tried to find corners where they could hide away, free from interference. But the rats pushed them out of these too: it was as though a tide of these rodents was flowing through the Park and engulfing it with their numbers.

The foxes, Badger, Weasel, Tawny Owl and Whistler tried desperately to keep them out of their own little enclave. But there was a limit to the number they could consume, any of them, including Owl's progeny, and they simply couldn't hold back the flood. When they saw the Hollow, their exclusive meeting place, become a nest for a party of rats, it was time to take more drastic action.

'It's war,' Weasel said bluntly. 'We shall have to fight to keep what's ours.'

Adder queried, 'Don't you mean "win back", Weasel? We've already lost the area.'

'Not entirely,' said Fox. The friends had gathered by his earth now that they had no specific place for a rendezvous. 'We still have our individual homes.'

'Just let them try entering my set,' Badger growled. 'They'll turn themselves into my larder if they do. But I'm worried about Mole. Could he defend himself?'

'Has anyone seen Mossy?' Fox whispered to the others.

Nobody had. 'I think a mole's best defence is his network of tunnels,' Fox said. 'If he stays deep underground he won't clash with rats.'

'We can't leave that to chance,' Badger argued. 'I shall have to go and see if Mole's all right, just to put my mind at rest.'

'How will you do that, Badger?' asked Leveret. 'If Mole's gone down deep how will he know you're looking for him?'

'Oh – um – we have a sort of signal . . . a particular call,' Badger informed him. He was making it all up. He didn't like to admit that Leveret had found a weak point.

'Look,' said Weasel impatiently, 'when are we going to teach these rats a lesson? We should drive them out of the Hollow for a start.'

'We'll begin tonight,' Fox said quietly. 'We'll round up every friend and relative we have. Then we'll descend on the rats in the dead of night. There won't be one left alive in this part of the Reserve if I have anything to do with it.'

'Bravo!' cried Weasel. 'I was beginning to wonder if we'd gone soft, but no! that's our Fox talking!'

Adder's red eyes glittered as he studied the resolute faces of the old companions. 'Just like old times,' he drawled.

— 10 —

Toad the Brave

There were many descendants of the Farthing Wood animals spread around White Deer Park. But those who had chosen to make their homes in the corner adopted by the original band of travellers now swelled the ranks of the fighting force led by Fox. Friendly and Charmer, son and daughter of Fox and Vixen, were chief amongst these. The animals moved towards the Hollow, silent and intent on their purpose. Any rat that crossed their path as they progressed was instantly felled. In this way sixteen had been killed even before they had reached their first objective. Tawny Owl meanwhile hunted tirelessly through the home woods, sparing no intruder. Holly guarded the chicks from raiders. Only the previous night a rat had been killed at the foot of the nesting tree. The owls too were fighting to defend their own.

In the Hollow the rats who had settled there sensed danger. The body scents of a large group of hunting mammals drifted across to them on the night air. They scurried into their runs and burrows and cowered there, hearing nothing and seeing only the quivering whiskers of a neighbour. The Farthing Wood band's silence was awesome. Not a sound escaped the muzzles of the animals, and their feet trod warily to avoid giving the alarm. Fox led them into the Hollow. He knew where

the rats' nests were. He began to dig with his front
paws. Vixen helped him. Badger, grunting with effort,
used his powerful claws to unearth the rodents, and
the rats shot out of their holes, flying in all directions.
The foxes pounced. Weasel snapped. Badger snarled.
Twelve rats were killed, though even more escaped.
The animals, however, were pleased with their work.

'The Hollow's ours again,' said Vixen.

'Yes, and it'll stay so now,' Fox vowed. 'We'll see to
that. But this is only the start,' he said, turning to his
companions. 'We'll hound those rats and harry them
and chase them and, if necessary, slaughter them wherever they are. All of us together. They'll find they can't
have their own way while we're around. Come on, my
friends. Let's sweep them away!'

While Fox's band concentrated on clearing their
favourite woodland area, another of the Farthing Wood
animals was trying to defend a different part of the
Reserve from the invaders. At the Pond Toad had
watched with horror as a mass of rats swarmed into
the neighbourhood, led by a particularly bold and burly
animal. These creatures seemed bent on creating
havoc. They plunged into the water and struck out for
the little islet in the middle of the Pond where the
colony of Edible Frogs liked to sit and talk to each
other. The frogs at once leapt for cover, diving to the
bottom of the Pond and its sheltering mud. But the
rats caught many of them as they struggled to get away.
The frogs were good to eat and the rats bit savagely at
them, killing some and maiming others. Then they
dragged their prey on to the little piece of land, fighting
amongst themselves for the best morsels. The big rat
Bully took the best pieces first. None of the others
argued about that.

The other denizens of the Pond, disturbed and frightened by the swarming rats, tried to get out of their way. Moorhens scuttled to guard their nests amongst the reeds. Coots rocked nervously on their platforms of weed and twigs as the water was stirred up by the sudden violent activity. As for the young frogs and toads, no bigger than penny pieces, who so lately had swum blissfully in the pond as tadpoles, they erupted in panic. An explosion of miniature amphibians, seeking desperately to escape the sharp teeth of the rats, occurred around the Pond's edge. The little froglets and toadlets jumped and leapt everywhere, landing sometimes amongst vegetation, sometimes on dry land, sometimes on top of each other, sometimes back into the water, and even into the eager jaws of the marauding rats. The Farthing Wood Toad, who had spent so many peaceful times on the shores of the Pond, couldn't bear to see this pandemonium breaking out. His stout old heart swelled with pity and indignation at his relatives' plight. He had no means of fighting the rats' onslaught. He was endowed with no sharp teeth or claws. But he remembered only too well the purpose of a nature reserve, and why White Deer Park had been designated as such. He couldn't sit by and watch the rats' desecration.

'Villains! Warmongers! Butchers!' he croaked at the top of his voice, hopping towards the seething waters in a fury. 'How dare you come here, destroying everything like this? Who invited you to this peaceful spot? You've no rights here. You're not fit to live amongst us. You're vicious and unclean and – and – poisonous creatures!' Toad was groping for appropriate adjectives. 'Filthy rodents who stink of – of – mess and slime. Leave those frogs alone! They're protected here by Man himself! This is their home! Get away from – ' Toad's voice ended on a choke as a powerful rat gripped him from behind. Toad writhed and wriggled in vain.

From the centre of the Pond, Bully sat up on his hind legs with a quizzical look on his face. In the darkness he scanned the shore with narrowed eyes. He was interested in, even amused by, the sole voice of protest. 'Who has the nerve to question what we're up to?' he asked roughly.

Toad was unable to answer him. His attacker's teeth had sunk deep into his neck. One of the other rats explained who was challenging them.

'A toad?' Bully whispered. 'Don't joke with me,' he warned the rat.

'It's no joke, Bully. Go and see for yourself.'

'I think I will,' said the other. 'This'll be worth seeing. A toad, eh? Well, this is rich.' Bully scrambled into the water and quickly paddled to the bank. He saw the immobilized victim who had dared to raise his voice to the rats. Toad's neck, badly bitten, was bleeding. The rat who had seized him now hastily let go as the foul taste of Toad's skin – his only defence against a predator – got to work. The rat clawed at its mouth in an effort to remove the evil taste.

'Who are you?' Bully asked, with a horrible rat grin that displayed his razor-sharp yellow teeth.

'The Farthing Wood Toad.' The reply was given in a gasp.

'The *what* toad?'

This time there was no answer. Toad's attacker repeated the title for him.

'Oh, so you're not a native of White Deer Park either?' Bully sneered. 'I've heard of this Farthing Wood and its clever animals who came here all in a group, helping each other on the way. You're well known all around, aren't you? But I don't see any of your friends around now to come to your aid. They must have abandoned you!'

'They'll come,' Toad managed to croak.

'Too late to save you,' Bully squealed with a leer. 'Pity really. I'd like to see how your Farthing Wood friends work together. You're a bit like us in a way. *We* work together, don't we, Brat?' He addressed his companion.

'Yes, we do, Bully.'

'Only – there's more of us,' Bully went on. 'That's the difference. We're going to control things. We've started already. We've needed a proper home – like you – for a long time. Now we've got one and we'll settle here for good. It's ideal, isn't it, Brat? Of course, we may upset some of you. We *are* rather grubby and hungry and greedy, too. But there's nothing poisonous about us. We're only too healthy, as you'll find out. We want the best for ourselves. It's natural, isn't it, Toad? You couldn't blame us for that. So you'll come to understand very soon what happens to creatures who object to our ways. And, with a bit of luck, your friends will understand as well, when they find you here and see how we deal with objectors.' He grinned again.

'Your threats mean nothing to me,' Toad answered painfully. 'I'm old and helpless. You'll gain very little from removing me from your path.'

'You'll be a lesson to others,' Bully sneered.

'I'm only a toad, a smaller animal than you. How will you tackle foxes and badgers?'

'We'll overwhelm them,' said Bully. 'Bigger creatures than we are will soon learn about the sheer weight of numbers. We're numerous, we rats, and very quick to multiply. More of us are coming. The Park will teem with rats!' He ended with a squeal of defiance.

Toad sank back, exhausted. Here was a grim picture of his beloved White Deer Park. This odious animal's prediction seemed all too possible. Dimly he saw a blur of white approaching from a distance. Deer were

coming to drink. Even they, the deer, would find themselves as strangers in their own Reserve.

'Shall I kill him?' Brat asked suddenly.

'No. You leave him,' said Bully. '*I'll* deal with this
bright fellow.'

Toad waited for the expected snap of the big rat's
jaws. He was fatalistic about his end and he watched
the animal's gimlet eyes rove over him. He felt almost
no sense of regret save that he wouldn't see his dear
friends again. One by one they came into his mind's
eye, those faithful, constant companions in
adversity . . . Fox, Tawny Owl, Badger, Weasel,
Adder, Mole. . . . Bully slowly opened his jaws. Toad's
jewel-like eyes closed. He thought of Vixen, Whistler,
Hare. . . .

There was a sound of many feet. The herd of deer,
unnerved by the presence of rats all around, had broken
into a run. They cantered towards the Pond. Some of
the rats were kicked, trampled by the mass of feet.
Most scattered. Bully looked up. The deer were huge
by rats' standards. There were not yet sufficient rats
on the ground to impede the progress of a herd of hinds
and their young. The big rat gave Toad a final warning,
scarring his body anew with a vicious lunge from his
teeth, before scuttling away. This time the rodents
withdrew from the Pond, leaving their victims dead
and dying behind them.

At dawn the next day Whistler flew from his roost in
a tall tree to the Pond to catch himself a breakfast. On
this occasion he found no rats; only the remains of the
night's carnage. The frog carcasses were strewn along
the water's edge and on the islet. Some floated on
the Pond's surface. The survivors cowered in the mud
underwater. To them the heron was a potential hunter
of frogs, although in fact Whistler had never caught

any of them. Whistler guessed at once who were the perpetrators of the killings and was greatly alarmed for Toad. He stepped amongst the bodies on his long thin legs, examining them closely and dreading to find a toad amongst them.

'No toad here,' he muttered with relief. He flew to the islet to look at the remains there but he didn't expect to see Toad amongst these as the place was almost exclusively the preserve of the frogs.

'The rats did it! The rats did it!' a coot called to Whistler. 'They were here, trying to spill us all from our nests. Only the deer stopped them.'

'They'll be back again, and what are we to do?' wailed the mother moorhen.

Whistler forbore to give an answer. The problem of the rats was becoming something far beyond what could be contained by hunting. 'Did you see a toad?' he asked worriedly. 'The one who often appears here – my friend?'

'Lots of toads visit the Pond,' the moorhen cheeped. 'I think I know the one you mean, though. He's a brave animal; he tried to stand up for the Pond's residents.'

Whistler was filled with pride. He knew this could be none other than the Farthing Wood Toad. It was so characteristic of him and all the Farthing Wood creatures. But now he feared more than ever for Toad's fate. 'Did he . . . did he suffer at all?' he croaked anxiously.

'We didn't see,' the coot answered. 'We had enough to do to save our homes and young.'

'I'd be surprised if he's still alive,' the moorhen said cheerlessly, 'when you see what happened to the frogs.'

The heron began a miserable search amongst the reeds and sedges. Toad had managed to crawl under cover after the departure of the marauders but he was too weak to call Whistler's attention. He watched the heron striding up and down, examining everything. At last the great bird came close enough for Toad to risk a cry.

'Here!' he gasped. 'Here, Whistler!'

The heron hurried forward. He saw Toad with his badly scored body. 'Oh! Oh!' the bird groaned. 'Toad, poor, poor fellow, what have they done to you?'

'Made . . . a mess of me,' Toad answered with difficulty.

Whistler bent his head down to ground level. He looked at Toad's wounds. 'You're – you're in a parlous state. Those are really deep lacerations.' The heron was so overcome by his friend's appearance he could hardly speak. 'I must help,' he muttered, more to himself than anything else. 'Whatever can I do for him?'

Toad provided the answer. 'Take me to the Hollow,' he whispered. 'The rats will . . . come back.'

'Of course, of course, dear friend, at once. But, will you be able to bear it? Would it pain you? My beak. . . .' His voice petered out.

'Better your beak than . . . a rat's fangs,' Toad murmured.

Whistler hesitated no longer. As gently as he could, he clasped the little creature in his bill. He tried to treat Toad as if he were lifting an egg and certainly he believed his old friend was just as fragile. With a couple of wing-beats Whistler was aloft and flying fast across the Park. Toad uttered no sound; he was beyond complaint. The Hollow showed up below. Whistler lowered himself toward it, hoping desperately that Toad could hang on. They landed, and amongst the soft vegetation Whistler cautiously opened his bill, placing his burden as comfortably as he could. He noticed the rat carcasses still lying where they had been felled the night before. In a rage he tossed every one out of the area so that

Toad alone occupied the Farthing Wood animals' meeting place.

'How do you feel?' Whistler croaked wretchedly. 'I do hope I haven't made things worse?'

There was no reply.

'Toad! Toad! Can't you speak?' the heron cried in desperation.

'Thank you,' Toad whispered, 'for rescuing me.' He gave a long sigh. Whistler's relief was enormous. Toad fell silent again. Then, with a final effort, he croaked: 'Tell the others I'm proud to have. . . .' His strength ebbed away. Whistler watched in abject misery as the brave animal gave up the fight. Toad, the discoverer of White Deer Park and the animals' guide during their long journey there, was dead.

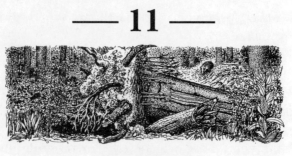

11

Battles

It was a mournful group of Farthing Wood animals who assembled after Whistler's distressing news. The heron had not yet recovered from his sad experience and he absented himself from the gathering. The friends stood silently in the Hollow, each lost in his or her own thoughts, as they gazed on their old companion. Adder was the first to speak.

'How small he looks,' he murmured, 'how soft and vulnerable. He never seemed to me like that when he was alive. I wish I had been spared this sight.' The snake was genuinely aggrieved. Expressions of regret were a rarity from Adder's lips and they made the scene all the more poignant.

'If only the humans had removed him instead of me,' Weasel said. 'He would have been well out of reach of any troubles.'

'Toad was never in the running,' Tawny Owl pointed out. 'The men were after larger game.'

'Why don't they come back?' Leveret moaned. 'We need protection.' He was of the opinion that Toad's death marked the beginning of a new dangerous period.

'For the moment they're more interested in the new reserve,' said Fox. 'The Warden has his hands full with two areas to oversee. When he comes to patrol around here again, he's in for an unwelcome surprise.'

'He'd better not delay too long,' Adder hissed, 'or he'll be patrolling a place called Brown Rat Park.'

The snake's sardonic words hung in the air with an awful portent. The animals actually believed that they could lose control of their home Reserve.

'We must fight and fight,' Badger urged. 'Warden or no Warden, White Deer Park must be saved.'

'How can we do that on our own?' Leveret demanded. 'We are so few and some of us, like poor Toad, have nothing to fight with.'

'We shall concentrate on our own corner, of course,' Fox told him. 'Vigilance is essential by night and day. We won't permit the rats to group again in our own territory. As soon as they approach, we strike. And we keep on striking.'

'What of the rest of the Reserve? Is it to be sacrificed?' asked Dash, who, more than any other animal, ranged the entire acreage.

'There are other fighting animals here besides us,' Fox replied. 'They too must battle to preserve what they have. The rats are a menace to each and all. We can't fight any battles except those for ourselves. We must all stick together in this small corner and defend one another. Until the Warden returns we are on our own.'

The animals were buoyed up by a renewed commitment to each other. They left the Hollow sadly but with determination that no more of their number should suffer Toad's fate. Vixen was the last to leave. As the others turned their backs and moved slowly away, she tenderly nosed Toad's body into a clump of fern where he was soon hidden from sight. She scraped some dead leaves around him. 'Whoever caused you to suffer,' she murmured, 'will regret it. You'll be avenged, I promise.'

Badger headed for the more mature woodland where
he had once had his set. It was close to the wreck of
his old den that Mossy had his network of tunnels.
Badger hadn't seen the mole for quite a while and he
wanted very much to reassure himself that the little
animal was all right. The old creature trotted along
with his rather lumbering gait, thinking dire thoughts
of what he would do to any rat that dared disturb his
friend. Badger noticed that the tree which had crushed
his old set still lay where it had been toppled by the
hurricane. He stood in contemplation. 'If I had been
at home when *that* happened,' he muttered, 'I should
be . . .' He didn't finish. He shivered. 'I'm lucky to be
alive still,' he told himself. 'I'm so ancient I sometimes
wonder how I've managed to survive for so long.' He
found one of the set's entrance holes still unblocked.
He worked his way inside and began to call out for
Mossy, whose labyrinthine system of underground passages interconnected at a nearby point.

'Mole! Mole! It's Badger! Are you there?' He stopped
to listen. All was quiet. 'Mole! Mole!' he wheezed
throatily. A fit of coughing overtook him. Badger
gasped and spluttered for breath. A scrabbling sound
was audible. Mossy was coming along one of his tunnels to investigate.

'Oh, Badger, it's you,' he cried joyfully as soon as
his long snout and front feet protruded from the end of
the passage. Mossy's eyesight was very poor but he
could smell the warm, comfortingly musty scent of
Badger's coat.

'Now, listen, Mole,' Badger said almost severely,
without any greeting, so eager was he to make the
smaller animals understand, 'you shouldn't come looking for intruders. Because, you see, I could have been
a rat, couldn't I?'

Mossy was amused. 'You a rat? That's silly.' He

tittered. 'I heard you calling me. At least – I thought what I heard was your voice and I came running. And now I see I was right.'

'Yes, yes, that's all very well. But you must keep yourself hidden. Don't give yourself away, that's all I ask. Rats are cunning, nosy creatures. And, given the slightest chance or hint of an opening, they'll barge in. You should block up this hole for a start.'

'If you think so,' said Mossy. 'I don't actually expect any rats to come searching for *me*.'

'No, no, perhaps not. I hope not, certainly. But they like to make their nests and so on underground and your tunnels would be ideal, wouldn't they?'

Mossy considered. 'Too small,' he pronounced. 'And too narrow.'

'There's no harm in being extra cautious,' Badger told him. '*I'd* be happier if I knew you would keep out of sight. I suppose there's no problem with food?'

'None.'

'Good, good. So you have all you need. Worms a-plenty, hm?'

'I've quite a stock of them. Would you like, perhaps, to – '

'No. No, I wouldn't.' Badger refused the offer he knew was coming. 'You'll need every last one. I'm not hungry. I just wanted to be sure you understand the difficulty and the danger we're all in. That's why I came.'

'Thank you, Badger,' Mossy said gratefully. 'I'll do as you say. Will you come again when the danger's past?'

Badger didn't know how to answer. He didn't think the danger *would* pass, unless the Warden returned to take control. The Farthing Wood animals were so few and the rats so many. He was very despondent but he didn't want Mossy to know this. 'How I wish we were still neighbours, so that I could keep an eye on you,' he said. 'I don't suppose you'd consider abandoning your run of passages and making some fresh ones along- side my new set?'

'Impossible,' Mossy replied. 'I have a family to look after. Didn't you know?'

'Oh!' Badger exclaimed. 'That's news to me. Of course there's no question, then. Well, Mole, you *are* a sly one. I really knew nothing of it. I do forget quite a lot, it's true, but I'm sure I wouldn't have forgotten that. Such an important thing too. I wish you well and I must stress once again, then, that you must be doubly careful.'

'You can depend on it.'

'I must go back,' Badger said. 'There's work to be done. I'll be back when the time is right; that's all I can say just now.'

'I understand,' said Mossy. 'Badger, do look after yourself. I ask you as you ask me.'

'Of course I will, my dear Mole. You can count on that. I've weathered every crisis and every storm that's come my way.' He thought of the fallen tree. 'I'm a – a *stayer*,' he emphasized. 'Yes, that's what I am.'

Satisfied that Mossy was in no immediate danger Badger hastened back to join the others. Fox, Vixen, Friendly and Charmer were hunting in a group, Badger was informed by Weasel. 'The rats are on the run here,' Weasel added. 'They're streaking away from this corner in droves.'

'Only to regroup elsewhere, I fear,' was Badger's comment. 'We mustn't let our vigilance slip for a moment.' He noticed blood on Weasel's flanks. 'But you're wounded, surely? Is it bad?'

'No, not bad,' Weasel assured him. 'We must expect to sustain some scratches and bites. The rats are fighters, I'll give them that. I had three of them hanging on me while I dealt with another one. I got rid of them all, though.'

'You killed them?'

'You bet I killed them,' Weasel growled.

'Good. The rats know we mean business. There's no-one like you for a scrap. I'll leave you, Weasel. I want to play my part in this.'

'Don't overexert yourself,' Weasel advised. 'You're not as nimble as you once were; none of us are.'

'I still have my teeth left,' Badger joked. 'That's all I need.' He vanished into the darkness.

Meanwhile Tawny Owl was making the most of the situation. As the foxes rooted out the rats and drove them before them, snapping viciously at the fugitives, Owl saw his opportunity. It was impossible for the foxes to catch all the rats as they fled, and the bird descended again and again, pouncing on the scurrying rodents with his outstretched talons. Some of the game he carried back to Holly and the nestlings. Some he left lying where they had dropped to feast on later himself. Just as the younger rats made an ideal food supply for his offspring, so did the larger, tougher rodents suit his own appetite. Holly was pleased with his efforts.

'You're a good parent,' she complimented him as she tore off mouthfuls to feed to her brood. Every so often she swallowed some of the meat herself. 'I always knew you were a great hunter when I used to watch you quartering the gardens for mice at Farthinghurst.'

Tawny Owl preened himself briefly. 'There's never been a glut of food quite like this,' he told her. 'We can all fill our stomachs many times over.'

'The youngsters are putting on weight nicely, aren't they?' Holly fluted, and then she was struck by a thought. 'You're taking food too, I hope? This is a tiring business for you, ferrying supplies to and fro, and we can't afford for you to wear yourself out.'

Tawny Owl was pleased by her concern. 'Don't worry about me, I can look after my needs,' he answered loftily. He thought of all the freshly killed rats he was going to eat and relished the prospect. 'I just take a morsel now and then, you know, between flights. Of course the little ones come first.'

Holly positively glowed after these words. What a selfless, diligent mate she had chosen! The wily Owl flew away with her praise ringing in his ears, full of glee at her ingenuousness. He sped to his larder on the ground and gulped down three rats, one after the other. 'Wear myself out,' he chuckled. 'There are no worries on that score, my beloved Holly. The day hasn't yet dawned when Tawny Owl doesn't manage to feather his own nest!'

Over the next few days the Farthing Wood animals pursued their campaign of ridding their home area of the rat infestation with some success. They began to see rats less and less frequently attempting to return to their own particular corner. Any rat that did put in an appearance was instantly removed. The foxes led the attack, night after night, never pausing to eat more than a fragment of food. Badger and Weasel backed them up, as did Tawny Owl, who, more than any of the others, continued to ensure that he enjoyed the fruits of his hunting forays. By day Whistler became an efficient ratter. The thought of Toad was never far from his mind as he patrolled the stream's banks to keep the watercourse free. Even Adder sought out the nesting females when he could and, if there were young in the nest, gobbled them up. Many a female rat too fell victim to the snake's poison. Adder's aim was to help reduce the rat population's potential to produce future generations. Sinuous, the she-viper, sometimes joined him in his expeditions. Throughout White Deer Park the hunting beasts and birds strove to save themselves and their territories from being overrun, yet it seemed that, as fast as they cleared one colony of rats from their midst, another appeared to replace it. It was as though all the rats from miles around were clustering with the sole intention of snatching White Deer Park from the rightful inhabitants.

12

A Chance for Plucky

Fox and Vixen had not forgotten their young relative in the other reserve. They had been preoccupied with the recent events surrounding Toad's death and the rats' appearance in the hallowed meeting place of the Hollow. However, Fox was conscious that Plucky had been left in limbo for too long. He cudgelled his brains to think of a way to get the young fox back to the Farthing Wood fold. At the same time Plucky himself had been active on his own behalf.

The Warden of White Deer Park had spent a lot of time overseeing the transfer of the excess Park animals into the new enclosure. This had come to an end and he was now principally interested to see how these creatures adapted to their new surroundings. He wanted to know about their nests and burrows and if youngsters were being raised. He wanted to know where they settled in this strange environment and how they spread themselves throughout the area; he wanted to know if they found food and, if they did, whether their diet was sufficient and broadly similar to what they had enjoyed before. His main object was to see that the animals, having been disturbed and removed from all that they were familiar with, were able now to accept this upheaval and, in spite of it, to continue to thrive. Plucky saw and easily recognized the man on his tours of the enclosure. The Warden visited each day, directly from his cottage, and Plucky took care to note where and when he entered this new Park.

The tall double wooden gates set into the enclosing wall were the very same through which Plucky and all the other animals had been brought by van. Here the Warden would open a little latch door set into the right-hand gate and step through, closing it behind him. Plucky was quite familiar with this procedure. He knew the little door opened on to the way home. The difficulty was that it was never left ajar. Moreover, a wide cattle grid was set into the road just a few metres from the double gates on the Park side. No creature had been able successfully to negotiate this. The grid was bordered by a low fence and there was simply no way to circumvent it. Plucky had pondered the possibility of leaping over the grid from the road but it was just too long a jump for a small animal such as a fox to perform. Then eventually another idea occurred to him.

Occasionally the Warden arrived not on foot, but in his Land Rover. Plucky was interested in this vehicle. He recalled only too well how he had been transported from White Deer Park in a similar sort of machine. He thought to himself that, if one machine could carry him, so could another. The Land Rover was usually parked just inside the double gates, which were then immediately closed behind it. Plucky knew that he could never reach the vehicle when it stood there, because of the cattle grid. But he had watched the Warden's movements so closely and so regularly that he was well aware that the man had to turn the vehicle in order to return home in it. There was only one turning point and this was on the other side of the cattle grid, where the fence ended and a flat stretch of grass verge made the manoeuvre very simple. Plucky, screened from view behind his usual vantage point – a thick mass of broom – thought long and hard about a way in which he could turn this manoeuvre to his own use.

One day, as he watched the Warden's habitual procedure with the Land Rover, Plucky noticed there was a way into the vehicle through the back, which was open. His heart beat fast with excitement. If only he could get himself inside, the Warden would do the rest for him: get him over the cattle grid, through the double gates and beyond the perimeter wall, where he could scramble clear and lie low until the man and his machine had disappeared. Plucky could think of nothing else, once this possibility of escape had presented itself. For days he kept to the same small area, noting the Warden's comings and goings, but never once did the man arrive except on foot. Plucky grew impatient. He continued to feed himself, drink when he was thirsty, sleep fitfully, but mostly he thought about Dash and all his other friends and relatives who he considered had all but abandoned him. And he longed to see the Land Rover again.

At last Plucky heard the unmistakable sound of a car engine one early morning while he was dozing in a dry ditch. He leapt up and cautiously moved towards the enclosure road. He saw the gates being opened. The Warden's Land Rover, its engine idling, was on the other side. The Warden drove through and parked in the selfsame spot as always. Plucky could barely contain himself. He tried to keep calm. He knew it might be well on in the day before the man completed his round and returned. He lay doggo; alert, tense and ready to make his bid for freedom.

Towards midday the Warden could be seen trudging back along the road towards his vehicle. Plucky wriggled as close as he could to the turning place without revealing himself. It seemed an age before the man was once more in his Land Rover with the engine started. Then the wheels slowly rolled forward, clattering loudly over the thick metal bars of the grid. The vehicle began its turn. As the back of it was swung round, Plucky, keeping close to the ground, ran forward. With the turn almost completed the driver accelerated slightly. Plucky knew it was now or never. A moment's hesitation and he would be too late. Just as the vehicle was about to re-cross the grid, the young fox galloped up and, taking a flying leap, fairly crashed inside the back of the Land Rover, sprawling on top of an assortment of objects. The fox was shocked and badly winded but he had one enormous piece of luck. The noise and jolt of his landing was naturally and very fortuitously obscured by the jarring and rattling of the wheels as they rumbled over the cattle grid again. The Warden was totally unaware of his passenger. He stopped the car. Plucky flattened himself against the floor, gasping and panting, as the great doors were opened and then closed behind him. The Land Rover began to move forward more quickly. A few moments later Plucky bounded free and half fell, half rolled, over the verdure of the open downland. He was bruised and battered but once more at liberty. The Warden drove on unsuspecting. A little later Plucky recovered, shook himself and set off for the boundary fence of White Deer Park.

Tawny Owl was looking very sleek. Holly remarked what a handsome bird he had become. 'Fatherhood agrees with him,' she told herself, and indeed, as far as his duties of procuring food were concerned, it did. Owl had acquired such a taste for rats that he rarely ate anything else these days. Every time he swallowed a kill he felt he was doing his bit for the community and so, of course, it was logical for him to swallow as many as he could. As he perched in a young oak, dozing in the sunshine as was his usual habit, Plucky re-entered the Reserve. The young fox had found Dash's scrape under the fence and had eagerly scrambled through. He longed to see his friend again and ran to the favourite spot where they had played together before their separation. Plucky barked Dash's name excitedly, expecting the hare to come bounding into view. But she didn't appear. This area was too distant now from the Farthing Wood animals' territory. Instead of Dash, Plucky found Tawny Owl, who awoke, grumbling about being disturbed by a fox's barks.

'Yap, yap, it's always the same with you youngsters; you've no consideration for your elders who might need a sleep more than you do.' He hadn't recognized Plucky. He was still in a semi-somnolent state.

'Tawny Owl!' Plucky cried joyfully, ignoring the bird's protestations. 'It's me, Plucky! Don't you have a word of greeting for your long-lost friend?'

Owl peered down, blinking his great eyes and trying to focus them better in the sunshine. 'Plucky? But you – I mean, how have you – '

'Escaped?' Plucky finished for him. 'I used my wits and the cunning I inherited. Oh, but it's marvellous to see you here and to know I'm back where I want to be, with all my friends. I'll tell you all about my adventure soon, but first, I want to know how things have been here. Is Dash safe?'

'Yes, Dash is safe,' Owl replied. 'But the Park has been overrun by rats. It gets worse and worse as time goes on, and one of our number, a dear old friend, hasn't survived.'

'Who? Who?' Plucky yelped anxiously.

'Toad. He was attacked and couldn't defend himself. He died bravely and the rest of us have declared war on the rat hordes by night and day.'

'Poor harmless, good-hearted Toad,' Plucky murmured sorrowfully. 'He never offered a threat to a soul. How glad I am I'm back in time to help defend our home. Are all our other friends still living?'

'Yes, thankfully,' said Tawny Owl, 'though I haven't seen a lot of them since I've been so busy hunting.'

'Have you caught rats?'

'Heaps,' the bird answered. 'My youngsters are insatiable and, naturally, I have to eat too.'

'You look as if you've done that all right,' Plucky observed. 'You've become rather portly.'

Tawny Owl drew himself up. 'I – portly? What nonsense, you cheeky young fox. I could hardly be portly when I've never been more active.'

But Plucky, though he forbore to say more, was right. The owl *was* portly and, as he accompanied the fox on his short journey home across the Park, Plucky could see how heavy Owl's flying had become, just as if his wings were scarcely sufficient to support him any more.

By day the rats mostly kept out of sight. Plucky, of course, was eager to begin hunting but he looked forward to his reception at his homecoming. He ran fast and Tawny Owl, puffing and blowing, battled to keep abreast. Fox and Vixen were overwhelmed by Plucky's return. Owl perched close as Plucky related how he had escaped from the other reserve.

'Ingenious indeed,' Fox said admiringly and congratulated his young relative. 'You remind me so much of Bold, your grandfather,' he said softly.

There could be no higher praise in Plucky's view. The tale of Bold's adventures and exploits in the outside world and his sad fate there had been part of the young fox's upbringing. Bold was almost as much a hero as the Farthing Wood Fox himself. 'You flatter me,' Plucky said humbly. He looked about him. 'I shall join your hunting party tonight,' he said, 'but now there's a particular friend I want to see.'

'No difficulty in guessing who that is,' Vixen commented. 'She's sure to be somewhere close by. I know you've both missed your games and races. It's a pity you've been separated so long, for things have turned very serious here since.'

'No time for play now,' Plucky acknowledged. 'More important matters for all of us to attend to. I – er – I'll leave you now, if I may. Dash and I were close companions and I'm impatient to renew our friendship. I only hope she hasn't forgotten me.'

'That day will never come,' Vixen assured him. 'She hardly talks of anyone else.'

Plucky, full of high spirits and keen anticipation, loped away to his longed-for rendezvous.

'A fox and a hare,' mused Tawny Owl. 'Such a strange sort of friendship. It could only happen amongst Farthing Wood animals.'

'You mistake them,' Fox told him. 'Dash and Plucky are White Deer Park animals through and through. Farthing Wood is only a name to them.'

'You know what I mean, Fox,' Tawny Owl answered. 'The place has gone but the spirit of Farthing Wood lives on here. And so it will, as long as we keep it alive.'

Fox was moved. 'Oh, Owl,' he said, 'how good it is to hear you say those words. It puts new heart into me.'

Plucky discovered Dash drowsing on her form in some long grass. He stood looking at her for a while, hoping she would wake of her own accord. The sun shone on her silky fur and a slight breeze was ruffling it. At last she opened her eyes and, at the same instant, sprang up and bolted. The image of a fox being the first thing she saw, she took instinctive action before there was time to recognize the animal.

'Dash, Dash, come back,' Plucky called disappointedly. 'Here's your old playmate back at last. Don't you know me?'

The hare had run quite a way before she turned and then raced back at full stretch. She leapt over Plucky in her glee, then jinked to right and left, her marvellously elastic body making Plucky's head spin. She butted him and tumbled him over and then she ran round and round in an ebullience of spirits so overpowering she couldn't check herself.

'Stop!' Plucky cried, delighted though he was to see her reaction. 'You're making me dizzy!'

Dash became still. 'Well,' she said, '*you* weren't carried out by Whistler. You must have been very clever indeed to arrange your own escape. And Plucky, I simply can't tell you how I feel. I've been lonely. The other hares are not exciting at all and, in any case, there's been no time to play or run or – or – anything, except to look out for those hateful rats. You must tell me everything. Did you dig under the wall, or learn to climb, or sprout wings or – '

'Let me get a word in!' Plucky begged. 'Then I'll soon explain.' Dash fell silent and watched the fox eagerly. 'It wasn't such a clever plan really, you know. I just thought I'd leave that enclosure as I entered it.' He described exactly what he'd done.

'It's brilliant,' Dash said. 'I don't care what you say. Even Fox himself never thought of your idea. Only you could have come up with it. I'm so proud you're my friend. I can't believe my luck. Hares are so dim-witted by comparison with you foxes. I wonder why I'm so fortunate?'

'We've grown up together, haven't we? We'll always be friends, no matter what else happens. We shall have our own mates and our own litters one day, but you and I will always have our own special relationship. Friendship's for ever.'

'Yes,' said Dash. 'Friendship like ours really is for ever.'

— 13 —

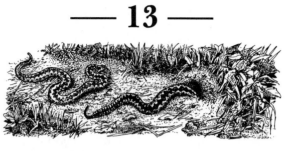

Bully's Cunning

The rats returned to the Pond. There was plentiful food here in the mass of froglets and toadlets hiding amongst the surrounding vegetation, and, led by Bully, a swarm of males and unmated females descended on the miniature amphibians and reduced their mass to a fraction of what it had been.

Bully smacked his lips as he crunched up the tiny prey. 'There's food to be had everywhere in this place,' he told some of his henchmen, 'if you know where to look. *We* know where to look, don't we? Nothing like a rat for digging up a meal somehow. And we need to feed up, all of us, so's we're strong and fast. Sharpen your teeth too, when you can, for the main assault. It's coming. We've got most of them on the run here but the main battle's to come. If we can push those old comrades back – back till they're cringing – we'll be supreme at last.'

'Who are the old comrades?' a young rat piped up.

'Who are they? Why, the ones who drove our friends out of that wood and thereabouts – on the other side of the Park. They think they're so almighty, the fox and the badger and the owl and the weasel – all their hangers-on – but we'll show them. We'll be able to raise such a horde soon that we'll drown them in bodies.'

'Dead bodies?' the young rat quavered.

'Don't be pathetic!' snapped Bully. 'What good would that be to us? Live bodies, live bodies, running all over them and pulling them down like wood ants on caterpillars. We'll advance through the wood, taking a tree at a time. Then we'll climb the trees, some of us on each, *many* of us on each,' he corrected himself with a sneer. 'Up and on to the low branches, see? *And* clinging to the trunks. They won't be able to reach us there. Then, when we're ready, and good and thick on the tree trunks, we'll drop down on them like wasps on rotten fruit.'

'You're a great one for allusions, Bully,' a big rat called Spike said. 'But from what I've heard, I wouldn't call the Farthing Wood animals rotten at all. There's nothing soft about *them*. They're tough and hard and cunning. Look at their leader. Everyone knows about *him*. It won't be so easy . . .'

'They're old, all of them,' Bully growled. 'Their fighting days are mostly behind them.'

'How have they killed so many of us, then?'

'We weren't organized, that's why. The others who went in – most of them females – were overawed in advance. They *expected* to be caught and chased and killed. They hardly fought at all. It won't be like that next time, I can tell you. I've got every bit as much wit and cunning as that fox.'

'How will we be safe up the trees with an owl picking us off?' demanded Brat.

'Yes, yes, the owl is a terrible hunter,' squealed the young rat.

'*Is* he so terrible?' Bully grinned at his junior. 'Have you seen him? He's so fat he'll soon be incapable of flying at all. Let him catch some more of us, yes, let him do it! The faint-hearted ones like you!' The young rat quailed. 'A few more of us in his stomach is all to the good. We'll weigh him down, ha ha! Even dead rats can be useful to my plan!' He leered at his astonished listeners. 'Make no mistake,' he said, 'we're going to tackle that precious band of compatriots. And we'll begin with the snake. I've heard enough about his insidious way of fighting. He only likes to seek out the weakest of us. Let's see how he enjoys fighting the strongest!'

'What if the humans come back?' Spike asked subtly. He knew no rat could combat their deviousness.

Bully didn't answer at once. It seemed as if he hadn't thought quite as far as that eventuality. Then he said in a whisper, 'They won't come back. Didn't we wait until we were sure they'd gone? And have we seen any of them since we came back here? Why would they come back *if they don't know we're here?*'

The other rats were silent. They weren't competent to give opinions on the ways of humans. Bully munched his way through another froglet, satisfied he had dealt with the doubters.

Adder's loathing of rats intensified after he saw what they had done to his old companion Toad. He couldn't forget how, at the end of each season, the pair of them had generally managed to choose a hole for hibernation that suited them both. It had been a comfortable arrangement. Now the snake was fated always to winter alone.

Adder could see that if the rats once gained a permanent foothold in the Reserve, the way of life for every resident of White Deer Park would change. The white deer themselves, or at any rate the timid hinds, were fearful for their fawns. They had no previous experience of rats and they suspected these scavengers to be lurking in the midst of every tuft of grass. Adder, always so close to the ground himself, was more aware of the rats' movements than most. He knew where many of the females had made their nests, and he set himself to visit as many of these as he could. The blind and naked rat young were defenceless against the snake's arts and, where the females tried to intervene, Adder's poison found its mark.

'Another strike for White Deer Park,' he would lisp as he slid from a nest, having eaten or otherwise disposed of the young who had been there. When Sinuous the she-viper joined him the pair of snakes made a potent strike force. Bully, however, was about to put a stop to this.

Information was brought to the big rat and his followers of Adder's sphere of activity. Bully decided to ambush the snake as he prepared to launch an attack. Despite the female rats' protestations (they never trusted the males near their helpless babies) Bully, Brat, Spike and a number of other males secreted themselves in a nest not far from a mossy bank where Adder loved to sun himself. They were confident of trapping him there and then ridding themselves of him for good. There was no doubt that Adder had done considerable damage to the rat colonies.

The squeaking of tiny rat nurselings was like a magnet to Adder and Sinuous. Their tongues flickered rapidly as they picked up the babies' scent. Red eyes glowing, the pair of snakes slithered eagerly through the undergrowth. Twigs and dry bracken crackled beneath their scaly bodies.

'Warm pink rats asleep in their den, not knowing that Adder is coming again,' the snake would hiss to himself in a sort of sing-song voice.

Sinuous augmented this humorously. 'A rat makes a break in the diet of a snake.'

Side by side they slid to the nest where Bully and his followers awaited them. Adder entered the run first. Inside the nest there was perfect silence as the nurseling

rats quivered in a mass, sensing the presence of a predator. The snake's long slim body was enveloped in
darkness. His busy forked tongue quickly picked up the
new odour of the male rats. He came to a halt. There
was danger here, he knew. He called behind to Sinuous,
'Stay outside! There's a trap for us!'

Sinuous made off in a different direction at all speed.
At the same time Adder, in the act of coiling around
in a circle to make his retreat, felt two pairs of jaws
clamp him in the middle. He instantly opened his
mouth and struck out with his fangs in the darkness.
Brat and Spike had seized him from the rear but
Adder's head was free and he endeavoured to lunge at
his other assailants to keep them at bay.

'Hold back,' Bully shrieked. 'There's death in those
fangs.' The other rats couldn't approach the swaying
mosaicked snake's head, which lashed first to the right,
then to the left. But Adder's long thin body was held
firm by the gripping jaws and, try as he would, he
couldn't shake them off.

'You've made one sortie too many, Poisonous One,'
Bully taunted him. 'You'll soon tire of your dipping
and weaving. We can hang on till you do. You'd like
to murder all our babies, wouldn't you? Well, you've
killed one too many!' Adder's head and neck continued
to sway from side to side. He was desperate to get his
venom into one of the ambushers and reduce the odds
against him. But he simply couldn't get close enough.

Sinuous darted through the undergrowth, alarmed
for her own safety and, believing the rats had already
disposed of Adder, she expected that they would soon
come after her. She had her own escape route under a
large flat rock, but this was a good distance away and,
as she shot towards it, she shuddered to think of
Adder's fate. There would be the most horrible revenge
taken, she was sure, on the creature who had dared to

lay low the future generation of the rodent horde. She had no connection herself with the Farthing Wood animals, other than with Adder himself, and the idea of trying to bring him aid from his friends would never have occurred to her. The snake was as good as dead already, in her own mind. However, by sheer coincidence, in her headlong rush towards the rock bolt hole, she slid under the very noses of Plucky and Dash, who were sunning themselves together on a high bank overlooking the stream.

The fox and the hare at first thought they were seeing Adder approaching them. But this snake had no battle scars on her body and no blunt tail. They jumped up as Sinuous came closer.

'What's the trouble? You're in a hurry!' Plucky barked.

The she-viper was aware this fox was one of Adder's oddly chosen acquaintances. 'The rats have turned the tables on us,' she hissed urgently. 'An ambush – back there. They've been studying our movements; how else could they have known?' (She was talking half to herself.)

'Is Adder caught up in this?' Plucky demanded.

' "Caught up" is the exact expression,' Sinuous told him. 'The rats won't let him give them the slip this time.'

'Tell me where he is,' Plucky commanded. 'He needs help.'

'I fear you're too late for that,' was the snake's response. 'But if you must go to see his demise, I'll tell you how.'

'Dash, run off and get the seniors – any of them,' Plucky ordered her. 'We need some support straight away. Now then,' – he turned once more to the she-viper – 'give me the directions without delay.'

'You're used, I suppose, to giving orders, are you?'

Sinuous commented cynically. She objected to this young animal's tone. Who was he to make demands of her?

'Oh, don't waste time with such remarks,' the fox said with exasperation. 'Do you hold Adder's life so cheap that you can't even put his rescuers on the right track?'

'I said I would,' the snake hissed crossly, and she did have a sort of fleeting regard for Adder's welfare; as much, at least, as was possible for a reptile of her independent nature. 'Go towards the slope and follow it down. Run through the heather to a bare patch of ground where the bracken shoots are beginning to uncurl. You'll see a small hole under a patch of bilberry. That's where he is.' She continued on her way at once, without pausing longer to see Plucky take the correct way. The sun-warmed flat stone, under which she could hide herself against the cool, dark earth, was an objective from which she didn't wish to be diverted for one more moment.

Plucky sped away, wondering at the cool blood of Adder's one-time mate. But he soon forgot about her in his vital race to the snake's aid. The rat hole was easily found. Plucky, of course, couldn't get into it. It was far too small for him. He put his muzzle to it. The smell of rats was overpowering. 'Adder!' he called sharply. 'Are you all right? It's me – Plucky. I've come to help!'

The snake, who was still fighting bravely to prevent any additional rats seizing hold of him, answered in a drone, 'I'm certainly not all right. Unless,' he added, 'carrying two large rodents on my back with their teeth transfixing my skin is a normal state of affairs.' Even with his life imperilled, Adder's naturally sarcastic temperament didn't desert him.

Plucky began to dig into the hole with his front paws,

scattering the earth behind him as he did so. Every so often he raised his head and barked loudly so that he could be located by Dash and any of their friends she might manage to find. The hole grew bigger and, very soon, Plucky could see some of the rats, who backed further into their run as they became exposed to view.

Pretty soon Bully, who had been dodging Adder's lunges, along with the others, could see that, with the advance of Plucky, the contest was about to dip to the rats' disadvantage. He tried a bluff. 'Keep your distance, young fox, and leave our nest alone,' he cried, 'or the snake dies!'

Plucky hesitated. He couldn't yet see Adder, who was deeper into the hole. He decided to bargain. 'Very well, let Adder go and I'll come no further. But if you don't, I'll dig you all out!' He turned and barked out his position once again, and Dash heard his call as she streaked across ground for more help. Plucky waited. There was no sign of Adder. Then the squeaking and squealing of the male rats as they discussed their position became very audible. Plucky knew they had no option but to release Adder and, once the snake was safely away, he intended to flush out every last rodent from the den. There was no place for sentiment in the animals' campaign against the rats.

'Stand back,' Bully suddenly shouted in his high-pitched rat's voice, 'so that we know there's no trick.'

Plucky moved a little distance off and Adder, bruised, angry, and with his dignity severely ruffled, emerged from the hole. His tough scaly skin had proved more of a barrier to the rats' molars than had Toad's soft warty hide.

'I'm obliged to you, I'm sure,' the snake had the grace to say to Plucky, who came and examined him solicitously. 'No great harm done, except to my pride.'

'That's of little consequence in these circumstances,' the fox remarked. 'How many attacked you?'

'Two. There were more who wanted to, though. I was able to ensure that they kept their distance.'

'Get yourself under cover,' Plucky advised. 'I'll deal with these scoundrels.'

Adder saw there was no more to be done for the present and, not ungratefully, slid away. Plucky crept back to the hole. The rats still chattered inside. Bully suspected the fox hadn't left the scene and told them to be quiet while he went and parleyed with the animal. He was clever enough to know that Plucky, as a member of the Farthing Wood group, was pledged to help the others in his community – and that all the Farthing Wood animals and their dependents had an unusual moral sense that made them susceptible to the idea of fair play.

Plucky saw the big rat emerge from the nest. Before he could pounce, Bully pre-empted a strike. 'Have the forbearance to listen to a rat for a few moments,' he began subtly. 'We're animals, too, young fox. We have our homes and our youngsters to look after. The snake came hunting for our babies. What else could we do but try to defend them?'

Plucky could find no argument to put forward against that. He said nothing.

'Why can't you and your friends, and me and mine,' Bully went on, 'come to a sort of pact?'

'Are you speaking as the leader of the rat invaders?' Plucky asked.

Bully bristled at the term 'invaders' but curbed his temper. 'I'm as much leader as anyone, I suppose,' he answered. 'Now listen. How would it be if we rats agree not to cross into your particular area? This is a big park: we can confine ourselves to the rest of it. We don't want these constant clashes; they do nobody any good.'

'I'm not in a position of authority to answer you,' Plucky informed the rodent. 'We didn't request your company in this Reserve. We've been content to live with our neighbours who were born here. I can only say all of us resent your intrusion and would like nothing better than for all of you to go back to your unwholesome haunts outside the Park. But, if you won't, we shall at least continue to defend our territories for as long as it's necessary.'

'You can't defend the whole Reserve, there aren't enough of you!' Bully snapped.

'I wasn't talking about the whole Reserve. We have our own area here where we have our dens and lairs, our nests and burrows.'

'Then you're agreeable to my suggestion?' Bully prompted. 'We leave you and yours alone. You do the same for us.'

Plucky had a pretty good notion that Fox and Vixen, Badger, Weasel and the others wouldn't be happy until the rats had been driven out of White Deer Park entirely, but he didn't want to lose the opportunity of securing, for the present at least, their own corner from the rats' encroachment.

'I'm not one of the Farthing Wood elders,' Plucky said. 'They make the decisions about such matters. But I can carry your message back to them and I think I can say that the idea of this kind of truce would interest them.' He didn't think this at all but he felt if Bully believed him, it would be to the animals' advantage in the long run.

'Take the message,' said Bully. 'We can all benefit from such an arrangement.' He felt a sense of triumph which he fought hard to disguise. With the assertive Farthing Wood animals out of the reckoning, he knew the rats had their best chance of building up their strength until their numbers could contend even with these legendary and formidable campaigners. He returned to the nest as Plucky left the scene.

Brat, Spike and the rest of the males clustered around Bully, demanding to know the details of his latest feat of cunning. With a leer as wide as it was sly, the big rat explained what he had gained.

'It's faultless,' he summed up. 'We can do as we please. The other hunters in this Reserve are a half-hearted lot compared to such adversaries as those.' He referred to Plucky and his friends. 'When we've reached our position of dominance, which is only a matter of time, we'll put my plan into operation to dispose of the last of the Old Guard.' This was how he designated the Farthing Wood compatriots. 'And, in the mean-time, we'll see that the snake, for a start, is out of the way. We know where he lurks. If an ambush wasn't the best form of strategy, a hunting party of our own can't fail to do the deed. We'll lose no more of our new-born to a reptile's stomach.'

Another Victim

Plucky's barks now brought answering calls from Fox, who had been alerted by Dash and was running with the young hare towards the scene of Adder's ambush. Plucky gave them a hasty rundown on the outcome, and then went on to describe how Bully had phrased his offer.

'He was a very big rat and definitely a sort of leader,' Plucky explained. 'He was directing events, I'm sure.'

'You handled the situation well,' Fox complimented him. 'It's useful to have a sort of truce for a while, because it gives a breathing space to those of us rearing young at this time of year to do the job properly. However, I'm not so naive as to believe that it isn't to the rats' advantage too. They're playing for time from some motive of their own.'

'The big rat mentioned babies,' said Plucky.

'Exactly. It's the same for them as for any. And I tell you, Plucky, once they're ready to move again, they'll be back to challenge us. They won't be content until we no longer stand in the way of their colonizing the entire Park.'

'How shall we stop them? We're so few.'

'I have an idea,' Fox said. 'It entails collecting together as many rat carcasses as we can find. Although I'm prepared to fight to the last drop of my blood to save White Deer Park and my friends, there are other measures which shouldn't be overlooked.'

Tawny Owl knew where a good number of rat carcasses were lying. This was because he and his family just hadn't been able to devour all of the prey he had caught. The owlets were almost fully fledged. They were greedy, healthy and strong. The youngest had gained on its siblings to some extent and now held its own. Holly flew on some hunting sorties herself. There was a distance between herself and her mate these days. Whereas she had once admired Tawny Owl's look of plump well-being, every time she saw him now he seemed to be a little fatter. She had no comment to make regarding his suitability as a provider. He had more than fulfilled his duty in that role, yet it seemed as if at the same time he himself had developed what she regarded as a gross appetite. Holly decided that, once the youngsters were out of the nest and fending for themselves, her connection with Tawny Owl need not continue.

Tawny Owl, for his part, had long ago ceased to regard Holly with anything more than mere tolerance, and his stock of that commodity was beginning to run low. He viewed her as a demanding, bossy sort of bird who, more by untoward circumstances than by his own choice, had become his consort. He forgot how she had nursed and pandered to him when he had been unable to fly, following a bad accident. He would never allow himself to recall that, at that time, Holly alone had kept him alive.

When Fox came to him for help Owl showed him the way to his dump of unused carrion. 'Magpies and crows have been picking at them,' he said. 'They're inedible now, as far as I'm concerned.'

Fox was amused. 'You certainly look as though you don't need to eat for quite a while,' he observed.

Tawny Owl scowled. 'Always the same cracks from everyone,' he grumbled. 'Weasel had the gall to call me rotund.'

'He could have said worse, I suppose. Flying is difficult for you now, it seems?'

'I'm all right,' Owl said. 'I don't need to travel far, do I?'

'You seem short of breath.'

'I *am* short of breath, dodging in and out of these trees to keep close to your level. I don't usually fly like this, you know that.' Owl was excusing himself. The plain fact was, he was enormously fat and heavy. 'Anyway,' he mumbled, 'that's quite enough about my problems, real or otherwise. What do you want these carcasses for?'

'I thought the Warden might be interested in them.' Fox looked at the bird with a meaningful expression.

'But where *is* the Warden?'

'In his den, I should think, fast asleep. Unless he's taken to nocturnal prowling like us.'

'I haven't seen hide nor hair of him for ages,' Tawny Owl remarked.

'No, but we must assume that he still lives in the same place.'

'And so?'

'And so, my stout old friend, we'll see what he thinks about a collection of dead rats littering the entrance to his home.'

Tawny Owl let the allusion to his size pass, preferring to believe the polite Fox was using a compliment related to his steadfastness. But he saw the subtlety of his friend's idea. 'Oh-oh, a noble plan, Fox,' he commented. 'The man's sure to follow this up.'

'That's what I'm reckoning on.'

'And an investigation will ensue.'

'I'm hoping so. Particularly if we can contrive to leave a sort of trail leading into the Park.'

'It's masterly,' Owl was pleased to comment.

'Well, it's a chance of drawing attention anyway,' Fox said modestly. 'Just as long as the man can spare some time away from that other enclosure.'

Fox rounded up Badger and Weasel, Friendly and Plucky to help himself and Vixen to port the rank-smelling carrion to the Warden's Lodge. He didn't suggest Tawny Owl put himself to the strain of carrying and Owl didn't volunteer.

The cottage was in darkness. Plucky leapt the low fence around the garden and placed one of the more fragrant of the long-dead bodies by a back door. The other animals left what they had carried at different points, making a sort of trail – as Fox directed them – leading along the garden and into the Reserve. They fetched a second load. Many of the carcasses were beginning to rot.

'Difficult to ignore those,' Badger said bluntly. 'All the flies from the surrounding area will be competing for a taste at sun-up.'

Bully lost no time in organizing a hunting party of the largest rats to dispose of Adder. Later that night, now they knew the Farthing Wood animals' guard was down, they set off at a run for Adder's haunt. They thought they would catch him asleep.

'Scout around here,' Bully told the others when they had reached the bank of sprouting bracken where Adder often could be found. Sinuous was woken by the scurrying rat noises. She slid from under the flat rock, thinking she had heard the pitter-patter of mice. She hadn't seen Adder again and had no way of knowing he had escaped. She watched for a sign of the mice.

She was hungry and an unexpected nocturnal meal would be very welcome.

The rats came closer. They bunched together now so as to be able to pounce at once at the first glimpse of a snake. Brat and Spike were in front, Bully to the rear. In the next few seconds Sinuous was spotted. At the same time she realized her error. The rats rushed her, thinking she was Adder. One snake was much like another as far as they were concerned. The she-viper struck at Brat, the leading rat, and her fangs pierced him through. But while her jaws were locked into her victim, his confederates seized her. All along her body, from her neck to her tail, Sinuous felt the sharp biting teeth of eight rats. Her poison soon immobilized Brat, but she was held so tightly to the ground she could not move a fraction. The rats gnawed horribly at her body, and this time they made no mistake. They thought they had Adder at their mercy. He was not to escape again. Gradually their strong teeth bit through the snake's body. Even in her agony Sinuous was unable to squirm, she was clamped so fast in the rats' jaws. The life ebbed out of her. Not until the rats were quite sure she was dead did they release their grip. The snake's mutilated body was motionless.

'He'll trouble us no more,' Bully growled. 'The babes are safe in their nests.' He showed no sympathy, not even a flicker of interest in Brat's carcass, which was now as lifeless as the poor snake's. 'We'll leave this area now until we choose to return to it. Let the adder's precious friends find him here and know now, if they never knew before, we're not to be taken lightly.'

The other rats mumbled and murmured amongst themselves. Some of them thought Adder's precious friends might not be content with merely having such knowledge. They were redoubtable fighters, all of them, and the rats reckoned they might have a thing or two to say and do after discovering a second victim from their community. First the toad, then the snake. . . .

'What are you muttering about?' Bully snapped irritably.

'We think the Old Guard, as you call them, will swear vengeance for this,' Spike grumbled. 'We may pay for this night's work.'

'What can they do?' Bully challenged him. 'Haven't they agreed to my pact?'

'How do we know that, Bully? The young fox gave no word.'

'*I* know it,' Bully growled. 'I know they need this lull, as we do. Don't they have broods to feed and raise?'

None of the other rats disputed any longer. They were eager to get back to their own nests and dens. They each had a store of food waiting which, in their mutual hunger, was beginning to call to them in a strident tone.

Ironically Adder himself all this time had been resting by the stream where he had first headed after his own tussle, in order to soothe his wounds underwater. His scratches and bites would soon heal and add their marks to the many others that decorated his black and white skin. Sadly the wounds inflicted on Sinuous would never heal; although Adder, coiled up by the water's edge, innocently believed that he had saved her from the rats' vicious attentions.

Early next morning the Warden's cat soon drew his master's notice to the stinking remains left on his doorstep. The man followed the trail of bodies into the Park, scratching his head furiously over the strange collection. He could think of no solution but he made up his mind there and then to carry out a thorough search of the Reserve for further clues.

The animals later saw him on his rounds. They were thrilled, each one of them, to see the man active once more in their Park. It didn't take a lot of consideration for them to arrive at the reason for his sudden reappearance.

'Neatly done,' Friendly congratulated his father. 'The man's picked up the scent.'

'There's many another message for him littering the ground,' said Fox, 'thanks chiefly to our overweight Owl.'

Vixen said, 'The poor bird has sacrificed his own homely comforts to our campaign. Holly will have nothing to do with him, he tells me.'

'Is he resentful?' Fox asked.

'No, he sounded remarkably cheerful,' Vixen said. 'Family life and responsibilities must come hard when you're no longer young yourself. The foraging, fetching and carrying quite wore him out.'

'Never mind,' Fox said jokingly. 'He can sit in a tree and doze the summer through. He has enough fat on him to last him to the end of the season!'

— 15 —

Frond

The animals were quite happy for the Warden to take control of events. They knew he was bound to find other traces of the rats' presence in White Deer Park. There were bodies sufficiently distributed around the Reserve for him to know some kind of battle had been raging. However, finding live rats was quite another matter. True to their habit of supreme caution and shyness whenever any evidence of human activity came to their notice, the rodents cleverly stayed under cover in daylight hours in the multitude of burrows and dens that they had established over the weeks. But the Farthing Wood animals felt sure this position could not be maintained for ever. Sooner or later one or other of the less experienced amongst the rat horde would slip up. It only needed a moment's carelessness for the Warden's and the rats' paths to cross.

Badger was glad of a rest. He had overlooked his great age for a while in the heat of the skirmishes but, now that there was a lull, he was reminded of it with extra force. One wet evening, as he prepared to go foraging for worms, a tremendous weariness overcame him. He sank down at the entrance to his set. His legs trembled. He let his head sink on to his paws. 'Oh dear,' he muttered. 'I feel as weak as a butterfly. This is the gallivanting catching up with me.' He glanced around in the evening light for a sign of one of his friends. Rain pattered down through the overhead canopy of leaves but otherwise all was still. 'I'd better rest for a while. Eating can wait,' he told himself. 'In fact,' he mumbled, 'I don't really feel hungry now at all.'

In the gentle evening shower Badger fell asleep, half in and half out of the entrance. Although he had slept throughout the day he simply couldn't keep his eyes open. His striped head and grizzled shoulders grew wet. His nether half, protected by the walls of his earthen tunnel, remained dry. Worms, slugs and snails, encouraged by the refreshing dampness of the wood, moved across the leaf-litter wood floor only centimetres from the badger. If one had crawled on to the old mammal's snout it is doubtful if Badger would have been aware of it. Soon his rhythmic snoring made a contrast to the pitter-patter of raindrops.

The rain began to fall more heavily after a while. Badger awoke with a start. He felt chilled. His old limbs ached with tiredness. He pulled himself on to his feet and sniffed the air. He looked distinctly shaky as he tentatively moved forward a step or two. 'I've certainly overdone it this time,' he whispered. 'What an old fool I am. And whatever did I think I was doing? It's as if I've been trying to recapture my youth. Ha! I lost that a long while back,' he told himself humourlessly. 'So far back I can't even recall what it felt like! Oh! I seem to have been old for so long.' His short legs had no strength in them. 'I just need a little more rest,' Badger summed up.

He waddled shakily back into his set. How glad he was that his home was now so close to that of Fox and Vixen. Should he need help they would be a great comfort. 'I mustn't worry them unduly, though,' the old animal decided. 'I don't wish to be a burden. I shall keep going for as long as I can. I'm glad I helped with the rats and did my bit, even if it's going to prove to be my last contribution. Oh, we've had such happy times together, all of us, and exciting ones too. Dear Fox, dear Vixen . . . and good old Owl. One couldn't have had better companions. Such staunch friends and allies . . . Adder and Weasel too . . . my, my, what a brave band we made.' He sank down in his warm sleeping-chamber, feeling especially drowsy. 'I must simply sleep for longer, I suppose,' he murmured. 'I need the extra rest. When I wake next time I'm sure to be much more refreshed. Oh dear, so old, so old. . . .'

Fox and Vixen were distant at this time, gathering what food they favoured amongst the tiny creatures drawn forth by the weather. Grubs, worms and beetles were easy to come by and Vixen pounced on a shrew. While they were absent from the home wood another animal, a stranger, entered it, looking for a resting place. She had been driven from her own territory by the abundance of rats. While not daring actually to attack such a large animal, they had, by their swarming presence, made her own home area uninhabitable. The animal was a young sow badger who had been brought up in what had once been a deserted set near the Park Pond. She was fully mature now and needed her own home. She paused by an entrance to the Farthing Wood Badger's set. She was attracted by the comfortable smell and promise of shelter. This was her main pre-occupation. Food wasn't a problem. She listened and smelt carefully at the tunnel. She heard Badger's snores dimly reverberating in the interior. She detected easily enough there was only one occupant. This in itself was strange – and even more so considering it was evening, when most badgers were abroad on essential errands. The young sow was curious and inquisitive. She took a few paces inside the set. One of her own kind would surely not drive her away. She would be cautious and respectful and friendly and . . . if the other animal was inclined to be friendly too, perhaps she would be granted a little niche of shelter as a temporary arrangement. She crept forward. The snoring was closer now.

In Badger's snug sleeping-chamber the young female found the ancient creature deep in sleep on his bedding of dry leaves and grass. She recognized his smell. She had encountered him before on his rambles around the Reserve and she knew at once who he was – the Farthing Wood Badger. But to herself and all the others of their kind in White Deer Park he was known simply as the Old Badger. She was delighted by her discovery. Badger's reputation was such that she knew she had nothing to fear from him – indeed could expect only kindness.

'I know you live alone and always have done so,' she said to the recumbent animal. 'My mother once offered you a share of our set. You were too proud to accept. Now it's the other way round. I wonder how you'll feel about a homeless creature begging for a place of repose in *your* home.'

It was a while before she found out. Badger's snores continued unabated for a time. Then, whether he had slept enough or whether he sensed some kind of disturbance, the old animal eventually stirred and at once detected her presence.

'Who's there?' he cried out, instantly alert.

'Only one who has nothing but the warmest regard for you,' the sow replied.

Badger sniffed the underground air vigorously. He didn't recognize her scent and he certainly wasn't familiar with her sound. 'What are you doing in my set?' he asked quietly without any accompanying challenge.

'Hoping for a shelter,' came the reply.

'From a little rain?' he chided her.

'No. From being made homeless.'

Badger digested this reply thoughtfully. He was only too familiar with the misery of being without a home, having been in such a position himself. 'Tell me how it happened,' he said gently. 'And – you may come in and settle yourself a little while you're doing so.'

'You're very kind.'

'Well, well, we'll see about that. What badger are you?'

'One from the once-abandoned set by the Pond. I'm called Frond.'

'I know that set. Are you – '

'One of the cubs whose mother once offered *you* shelter,' she anticipated him.

'Yes. I thought so. You're welcome then, for a spell, for the sake of that gesture,' Badger told her. 'Now tell me your story.'

'Easy to tell. My family have all dispersed. We were ousted.'

'By the rats?'

'Yes,' Frond said sadly. 'The pressure was impossible to withstand. They simply overran us.'

'I understand and you have all my sympathy. We've had our brushes with rats, too, but you'll have some peace here, at least for a while. We have a sort of uneasy truce with them.'

'The "we" being you and your fellow travellers from that distant place?' Frond summed up.

'Yes. You know about us?'

'Of course I do. Doesn't every creature in the Park? I know you're the Old – I mean, the Farthing Wood Badger,' Frond corrected herself in mid-speech.

Badger was tickled by her slip of tongue. 'Oh yes. I *am* old,' he grunted. 'So old I can't even collect my food tonight.'

Frond eagerly offered her services. 'Please let me

help you,' she begged. 'In return for the shelter you're offering me, the least I can do is to bring you something to eat. Are you quite unable to move?'

'Not quite,' Badger answered. 'But I'm very, very tired.' He enlarged on the brushes with the rats. 'Did too much, you see, Frond,' he finished by saying. 'Forgot my age. Now I only want to sleep.'

'I'll go at once,' Frond told the Old Badger. 'I'll bring you back enough for a feast; you wait and see. And for the moment I'll disturb your slumbers no more. I hope you'll forgive my intrusion but – oh! how glad I shall be to rest free from those scurrying rodents.'

Frond's diligence in her task of foraging kept her active well after the dark hours. She was collecting such an assortment of delicacies that it was doubtful if a whole family of badgers could have eaten it all, let alone one weary and ancient animal with a waning appetite. She took her catches to the foot of a tree, a little at a time, returning regularly with fresh contributions so that the pile grew and grew. In the early morning light, unknown to Frond, a pair of onlookers watched her proceedings with interest and commented to one another.

'Whatever can she be doing?' Dash asked her favourite companion, who, until a few moments previously, had been enjoying a game of something like hide-and-seek with the young hare.

'Food-gathering, of course,' Plucky said. 'But not in a way I've ever seen our Badger do it.'

'Where has she come from? I've never seen her before. Shall we speak to her?' Dash continued in her curiosity.

'Let's watch for a bit longer,' suggested Plucky. 'I'm interested to see what she's going to do with all that food.'

The young sow badger returned to her dump with some plump roots of wild garlic she had dug from the wet soil. She examined the miscellaneous assortment and appeared to think there was sufficient. Then she picked up a wriggling knot of worms in her teeth and set off along the short distance to Badger's set entrance. Plucky and Dash were astounded.

'This is very strange,' said the fox. 'She's actually going inside Badger's set! Where is he? He can't have vacated it!'

'He's not – he's not – ' Dash couldn't say what was in her thoughts but Plucky understood well enough.

'Surely not!' he whispered. He looked thunderstruck. 'We *must* find out. Come on, Dash.'

As they galloped to the set, Frond emerged again from it and, seeing them rush towards her, stood stock still.

'Where's Badger? Where's Badger?' Dash shrilled.

Frond backed a couple of steps, feeling herself under threat. 'He's inside munching the worms,' she answered tremulously. 'He's all right. I'm trying to help him, really I am.'

Plucky and Dash skidded to a halt, relief flooding over them. 'So the pile of food back there is for him?' Plucky guessed.

'Of course. He's very weary and, since he's being kind to me, offering me shelter, I'm doing what I can to repay him.'

'But I – we've never seen you before,' Plucky remarked. 'How long have you known our Badger? How long has this arrangement been running?'

Frond relaxed and answered brightly, 'It's only just begun.' She explained how she had arrived in the wood and discovered what she had believed at first might be an empty set. 'Are you Farthing Wood animals too?'

'No. White Deer Park born and bred,' said Plucky,

'but related.' He looked at her approvingly. 'Badger should consider himself lucky,' he commented, 'to have such a young and willing helper. You've collected enough food for him for days.'

'I hope so. I don't think he should move much for a while. He's quite plainly exhausted himself. But, of course, I have to eat too, so my efforts are not entirely unselfish. Anyway, I'm more than happy to do whatever I can for him. It's hateful to be without shelter. For a creature who's used to being solitary like the Old Badger, he's being very generous to me.'

'He's not solitary,' Dash protested. 'He has a host of friends.'

'But he's never shared his home before,' Plucky reminded her. 'Well, give the dear old fellow our greetings,' he said, turning again to Frond. 'Tell him Plucky and Dash wish him soon amongst us again.'

' "Plucky and Dash",' Frond repeated. 'Nice names.'

'What's yours?' Dash enquired.

'Frond. I hope *we* may be friends.'

'I hope so too,' said Plucky.

Frond turned to pick up more food. Suddenly she froze. 'Look!' she hissed.

Under the trees the tall figure of the Warden approached slowly. He was searching every step of the way for the source of those pests left so conspicuously on his own threshold. He carried a torch which he swept over the ground. Its beam raked every metre of the wood bottom for a clue, first in this direction, then in that, then in yet another. Plucky knew at once what was the man's purpose. Before the three animals scattered he said with satisfaction, 'Fox's ruse worked. He set something in train that won't end until the rats are rooted out to the very last one.'

16

The Poisoned Bait

It wasn't quite that simple. To begin with, the Warden's checks had so far only brought to light more dead rats. He knew perfectly well that if there were dead rats in the Park, there would most certainly be live ones too. But tracing them was another matter. He contemplated putting out dressed bait, but the difficulty with that was that grain or seed might attract the wrong animals, and the last thing he wanted was to poison small creatures such as voles and wood mice and shrews, whose existence in White Deer Park he wanted to safeguard. It was a knotty problem. He knew rats, generally speaking, liked to nest in the vicinity of water. He had made evening excursions to the stream-side and to the Pond but had never managed to be around when any of the rats were drinking. He had a feeling that the rats had infiltrated the area of White Deer Park when his interest had been principally with the new reserve, and he blamed himself for not being more circumspect. His ambition was for the two reserves under his jurisdiction to be united, and nego-tiations with the owners of the intervening land were at an advanced stage. But, before that highly desirable object could be attained, the Warden knew that White Deer Park must be cleansed of any threat of disease.

His searches continued without success for some

days; then, at last, just as the Farthing Wood animals had conjectured, a young rat crossed the man's path in a reckless evening excursion for food. The Warden was able to avoid detection by the animal long enough to trace it to its nest. Now there would be some point in baiting the rodents. He thought it unlikely smaller animals such as mice would wish to approach a rat colony, where they would very probably be attacked. So it would be safe to leave some grain close to the nest since only rats would be likely to give it any attention. The man lost no time in making the necessary preparations. His cottage was only a short distance from where he had sighted the careless rat and he suspected this nest was the source of the rat carcasses discovered near his home. He couldn't wholly account for the collection of dead rats in his garden and could only surmise they had all suffered from eating items disagreeable to the rat stomach. In fact the whole episode was really a mystery to him.

The poisoned bait was destined to achieve nothing. The Warden was unlucky enough to have traced the very colony where some of the most experienced rats of the entire horde were, for the moment, making their homes. Amongst these was Bully, and he was all too familiar with every human endeavour to combat his own kind.

The young rat whom the Warden had spotted running over ground was the first to find the tempting receptacle of grain. He had the sense to report the strange object to Bully, whose whiskers twitched angrily as he listened.

'Leave it untouched,' the big rat shrieked. 'All of you, listen to me. The humans are on our trail. They'll put down all kinds of innocent-looking items with the most delectable appearance, the most appetizing smells, even. I tell you, these things are DEATH! We don't need any assistance from our kind, interested humans, do we? We can look after ourselves, can't we? And I tell you (and you know I have the requisite knowledge) that, so long as we ignore any cache of food that appears suspiciously suddenly in a place where the last time you looked there wasn't anything, there is nothing they can do to us. No, nothing! We've been battling with humans through the ages and, don't you think, in all that time, we haven't learnt a thing or two? Oh yes, my friends. We know all about their cunning, sly tricks. But we have cunning, too. And that's why we'll evade every measure they take. Trust me, friends, we have the measure of them. Take the word round to be on guard. Now, more than ever, we mustn't slip up. It's almost time for that last big push that's going to see White Deer Park fall into our grasp.'

So the poison failed to do its task. It lay untasted where it had been put and the rats continued to thrive. Youngsters in the various colonies were growing fast and Bully watched their progress with keen satisfaction. Soon the adult numbers would be boosted by this new generation – young, well-fed and strong – and then there would be no need to hold back any longer.

The Warden shook his head over the state of things. How was he to get to grips with the threat? From the number of dead rats he had discovered around the Park, he knew that the resident animals were fighting the unwelcome strangers: fighting for space, for food supplies, for their homes. He was deeply concerned about his charges' welfare. The white deer themselves were just as much in danger as the rest. Now he must fight, too, to protect and preserve the Park from calamity. The situation required urgent and specialist action, but he would need to know that an extermination squad would be able to operate without putting the lives of the Reserve's rightful inhabitants at risk. Would that be possible? The Warden fretted over the dilemma. And while he fretted, the animals of Farthing Wood had relaxed in the lull in fighting, consoling themselves with the knowledge that the man in whom they had such faith was putting matters to rights.

It hadn't taken Adder long to discover the mutilated body of Sinuous, because the hole under the rock was one of his own places of concealment, to which he returned frequently. He was shocked by the sight of the dead she-viper. He knew at once what had occurred: there was the body of the dead Brat beside her! He was horrified to think that in some way he himself was to blame for the event. His discovery was made even more horrible by his belief that he had made Sinuous safe at the time of the ambush. She had been saved from that, only to invite the rats' revenge upon herself later. Adder knew the attack had been meant for him and he felt a double sense of guilt because he had escaped while Sinuous had been killed.

'I'm to blame for this,' he hissed. 'She had no quarrel with rats, except through our friendship.' It was a word he didn't allow himself to use often, preferring not to admit of any real feeling for a fellow creature. That was the snake's way. But first Toad and now Sinuous were lost, and Adder's sorrow on these occasions had been unfeigned. In a way his feelings surprised himself. He began to realize that previously he had been putting up a front that had had some elements of sham about it. He stared at the still body. 'I mustn't talk about this,' he lisped morosely. 'It puts me in a bad light. The others will think I deserted Sinuous, which I never intended to do. Oh, those evil rats! It would have been better if they had really vented their anger on me – as

they thought they had. It was I who had declared war
on them, not she.'

He kept apart from the other Farthing Wood animals, remaining alone and dispirited. His own wounds
healed. A bitter anger glowed in his reptile's heart
for the rats' deed. He knew there must come a final
confrontation and, when it did, he wanted to be in the
thick of it. He would go down fighting, along with the
friends left to him; for he was of the opinion that all
their days were numbered and that, in due course, only
rats would dwell in what had once been called White
Deer Park.

The other animals remarked on Adder's continued
absence. Could anything have happened to him?

'He was certainly hurt in the rats' surprise attack,'
Plucky said. 'He's probably lying low.'

'We've none of us taken it upon ourselves to find out
if he was all right,' said Fox. 'I'm worried about the
old rascal and I don't think we've served him very well.
He must be feeling like an outcast.' In some way this
was true, but not in the way Fox had suggested. 'I'm
going to look around for him,' he decided aloud. 'Does
anyone want to join me? I know Vixen will.'

'I'd be pleased to do so,' Plucky volunteered
promptly.

'What about you, Weasel?' Fox asked.

'Oh yes – by all means, if you really think that – er
– he could be suffering.'

'Don't inconvenience yourself,' Tawny Owl retorted
sarcastically.

'I didn't hear you putting yourself forward,' Weasel
snapped.

'I don't need to,' Owl replied loftily. 'Fox would
know I'd make one of the party automatically on such
an occasion.'

'Really? That's not what I remember,' Weasel disputed. 'I can recall remarks about freelance days being over and talk of new responsibilities as a father and so on and so forth, just as though none of the rest of us had ever had such concerns.'

Tawny Owl glared at Weasel but was, for the moment, short of an answer. Then he shook his feathers and said, 'That situation has come to an end. The fledglings have left the nest and Holly – well, Holly. . . .' He shuffled on his branch awkwardly.

'Holly has turned her back on you since you've grown fat,' Weasel finished mischievously.

'All right, Weasel, don't let's squabble,' Fox intervened. 'We should be glad that we have Owl back in the fold, though I hope, Owl' – he spoke politely to the bird – 'your differences with your partner will soon be resolved.'

'Don't care if they're not,' Owl said childishly. 'I did all I had to at the time. Now I'm free again, that's all.'

Fox deemed it was time to change the subject. 'No good hoping for Badger's company,' he remarked.

'None,' Weasel agreed. 'He has the perfect excuse to stay at home, with a young animal ministering to all his wants.'

'And a female at that,' Tawny Owl said archly.

None of the others thought anything of that, and Owl's attempt to be coy fell flat. He tried to regain some ground with another quip. He hooted, 'It could be described as a case of feathering your own set!'

Badger had not set out to benefit himself but it was undeniably true that his comforts were being catered for. When Frond had brought him that first mass of writhing earthworms, Badger had thought initially it was all she was bringing, and indeed it would have been enough. 'Worms, choice worms,' he commented cheerfully. 'You're very good. My appetite is kindled again.' But, even as he began to eat, she disappeared and, shortly afterwards, returned with bluebell bulbs and roots of another plant. 'More? For me? You're really too kind, my young friend. But I don't know if – ' His voice faded as he watched her vanish again. Intending to show appreciation, rather more than actually wanting to eat, Badger chomped his way through a selection of roots, only to find additional provisions were still being delivered. 'Honestly,' he commented with his mouth full, 'you needn't . . . go on with this just now. You see I . . . can't always . . . do justice to everything you want me to. . . .'

'You rest comfortably,' Frond said softly. 'I'll collect the last from my pile. You don't have to eat it all at once, and maybe there will be enough for me. And then I'm going to gather some fresh sweet-smelling bedding. I'm sure you'd welcome it. It's a bit musty in here and I want you to be free from worrying about renewing it yourself. It's time an old creature like you had some home comforts.'

Badger sank back with a sigh as Frond departed again. Curiously enough, the independent old animal didn't raise a murmur of protest. He rather liked the young sow fussing over him and, despite his great age, couldn't but be aware of her charm. She was a generous-hearted and affectionate badger who was genuine in her concern for his welfare. Badger began to revise his original idea of Frond making only a temporary stay in his set. His extreme age made him wonder if he would indeed be capable of looking after himself in the future and, if not, then Frond's unexpected arrival was providential. He didn't want to quit the scene just yet. The fate of White Deer Park was in the balance and he wanted to be around when the issue was settled. He wanted to see his friends win back the Park from the invaders, with the Warden's help. He wanted to

know all was safe and secure before he . . . before
he. . . .

'Here, Old Badger,' said Frond, returning backwards
into the sleeping-chamber, dragging the fresh bedding
with her. 'You'll sleep sweetly on this. It's grass to
make you dream.'

'I'm very grateful to you,' he said. 'Take some for
yourself. You can take your pick of sleeping-chambers
too. I've only used a small proportion of this set's area.
My friends Mole and the foxes dug most of it for me,
you know.'

Frond listened in wonder. The Farthing Wood animals' penchant for helping one another had acquired
almost mythical status in the Reserve. She thought it
a beautiful and noble trait. 'You must please tell me
all about it,' she breathed. 'I've met some of your
friends. Tell me about all of them and how you live
and enjoy each other's company.'

'I shall do so, of course, with the greatest pleasure,'
said Badger. 'And I hope my friends will become your
friends. We need, all of us, to show solidarity as never
before against our common foe.'

The search for Adder got under way. He was sought
in the usual places. Weasel found the dry remains of
Sinuous under the flat rock, and the animals could only
guess at Adder's feelings. They consulted Whistler over
the snake's disappearance. The heron once again haun-
ted the shallows of his beloved stream. Young fish were
beginning to appear in the waters and the bird had
high hopes of it returning to its halcyon days as a
hunting ground.

'I really can't recall when I last saw Adder,' Whistler
said dubiously. 'It seems an age. It's very sad that none
of you know where he is. The rats are vindictive and

vicious. I do hope *they* have no idea where he's gone to ground.'

Fox explained about Sinuous. 'They may think they have dealt with him already,' he surmised. 'If only we knew! If Adder's being pursued, why doesn't he come to his old friends for protection?'

'Too proud for that,' Tawny Owl remarked. 'Whistler, how's your rheumatism?'

'About the same,' the heron replied. 'And you? You're looking very – '

'I don't wish to know how I'm looking,' Tawny Owl broke in petulantly. 'It's immaterial, isn't it? We're debating the disappearance of Adder.'

A wry look came into Whistler's eyes. He stepped sedately to the weeping willow where Owl was perching. 'I humbly beg your pardon,' he said courteously in his old-world manner. 'I hope you'll allow me to say, however, that I'm delighted to see you in such good health.'

'Oh! I see,' Owl bumbled, greatly mollified. 'Very good of you, Whistler. You're most polite, I'm sure.'

'When this exchange of pleasantries finally comes to an end,' a well-known lisping voice sounded from the undergrowth, 'I shall be ready to give an account of myself.'

'Adder!' the friends cried together.

'None other,' said the snake as he slid into view. He had heard the remarks of concern as to his safety from his hideaway in the scrub and was secretly relieved. How glad he felt to hear his friends' voices again and to feel free to end his period of isolation. They made much of him and the old rogue remained as impassive as ever under their expressions of welcome. 'I have some news to give you,' he drawled. 'The Warden is powerless to aid us without killing innocent parties.' The canny reptile knew all about the rat poison. 'He won't know how to act, and the rats are preparing for their final onslaught.'

17

The Battle Rages

While the Warden racked his brains as to the best course to adopt, taking advice from every expert on the subject, the Farthing Wood animals held themselves ready in the strange lull for the expected showdown. The band of friends was complete and none strayed far from his fellows, taking immeasurable comfort from this united front. None of them knew if they would survive the battle that was coming. Each felt that to lose his life would be preferable to living a hole-in-corner existence amid a sea of greedy, alien and dangerous rodents.

Bully saw the day approaching fast when his long-laid plans could be brought into effect. He was impatient for action and, in the end, his eagerness got the better of him.

'The horde must gather,' he squealed to his henchmen of the colony. 'The whole mass, you understand? We strike by night into the wood of the old comrades.'

'The Old Guard?' Spike queried. He was open-mouthed.

'That's what I said!' Bully snapped. 'And let me stress the word "old" once again. Because that's what they are, these precious fighters – all of them!' (He didn't consider the younger generation of animals, descended from the original group.) 'We'll catch them unawares, like I said,' he went on. 'They won't be expecting us so soon! They think this lull in fighting I arranged so shrewdly is still operating. But we'll show them otherwise, won't we?'

'Shouldn't we wait until our youngsters have grown to their full potential?' Spike asked. 'We need maximum strength, don't we?'

'We've got maximum strength,' Bully growled. 'We're more numerous than any species in this Park. We outnumber *all* of them. What should we wait for? For the humans to devise some subtle new poison that'll catch out those stupid ones amongst us?' He glared at Spike as though he was included in that category.

'Of course not,' Spike answered sullenly. 'When do we go, then?'

'As soon as we're massed together,' Bully answered. 'Then we race for the far corner. Wave after wave of us. We'll swarm up the trees. We'll carpet the ground. By tonight the old fogies will be overthrown. We'll have them running in every direction.'

Spike wasn't quite so optimistic as the impetuous Bully. But wisely he held his tongue.

Under cover of darkness rats from all over the Park assembled close to Bully's own nest. They were content to leave him to co-ordinate their actions. He was generally assumed to be the cleverest and the most ambitious amongst them. It was a particularly dark night. There was a lot of cloud cover. Bully took the lead. The others followed. Together, like ripples of a tide, the rats surged silently and purposefully to their goal.

Bully stopped short of the actual growth of woodland he believed sheltered the animals of Farthing Wood and their homes. He was cautious, and secrecy was imperative. He directed some of the smaller males to scale the first trees on the outskirts. He wanted the biggest, strongest animals to penetrate, along with himself, deep inside the wood, with the trees behind them well guarded by their clothing of rats. The rodents took up their stations, some swarming up the trunks and lying low across the branches, others clinging to the trunks themselves. From here they would drop on anything that moved underneath. Thus the environs of Fox and Vixen and Badger's wood were covered, a few metres at a time, whilst the vanguard of the rats under Bully pressed on determinedly.

They encountered no challenge. Even Bully was surprised. There was no hindrance at all to their continued movement.

'You sure this is the place?' Spike grunted.

'Do I make mistakes?' Bully snarled. But, despite himself, he was beginning to have doubts. Where *were* the Farthing Wood animals? Could they have been forewarned? Were they expecting the rat horde? Had they laid their own plans?

Suddenly one of the big males hissed, 'I see movement ahead!'

The rippling tide came to a halt in dead silence. Whiskers twitched nervously, excitedly. Feet quivered. Hundreds of pairs of eyes pierced the darkness. An animal smaller than the rats themselves scurried through the leaf litter in quest of food. It was a mole – a purblind, innocent creature running alone before the enemy host.

'Kill it!' hissed Bully.

Spike ran forward. The mole, whose hearing was good, spun round. It was Mossy, making his first venture above ground for a long time. The big rat was upon him in a trice. The little mole squealed in terror, but Spike quickly ended the pathetic sound. Mossy's cry was cut short and his little black velvet body cut down, but not before an owl, coasting over the tree-tops, had become witness to the event. Tawny Owl's mate, Holly, flew closer to investigate. She saw only too well the massed ranks of rats, and, veering in her flight, flapped swiftly away to give the warning. Bully had taken his cohorts into the storm-damaged wood where Badger had once had his set. Mossy's home was there, but most of the Farthing Wood animals now congregated in the neighbouring copse where Fox and Vixen had always had their earth. Holly flew straight to Tawny Owl, their past differences forgotten. Before he could register his astonishment she screeched: 'They're coming! The rats! They're coming! An army of them!'

Tawny Owl heaved his bulk into the air and called repeatedly, 'Make ready, make ready! The enemy is approaching!'

Fox, Vixen and Weasel emerged and rushed to the point they had long ago decided was their first defence. This was a thick stand of holly scrub, almost impenetrable, behind which they could shelter. Before them was a gap in the woodland where the open ground which the rats would have to cross was in full view. Here the friends could not be outflanked. The other foxes came running: Friendly, Charmer and their mates, Plucky and all the relations of Fox and Vixen who populated that hereditary quarter of the Reserve. Leveret and Dash, Whistler and Adder all came, some for support, some for protection. Frond came from Badger's set and settled herself a few paces before her new home, grimly determined to defend the old creature at all costs.

When the first victim fell to the rats' concerted campaign – poor Mossy – it goaded the rodents into a mad rush forward. Bully couldn't check them. The impetus of their charge carried them deeper into the wood. Still there was no challenge. Now Bully guessed he had miscalculated. It was too late to hold back the mass movement. The rats posted amongst the branches were left behind, not knowing they were in the wrong place. They were forgotten as the surge swept on. Bully tried to contain the rush but he was carried along with it, still in the vanguard with Spike alongside him. 'Ease up!' he shrieked. 'This is a surprise attack. We're giving the game away!' But it was too late to stop them. The rats poured on like a flood. Small animals like voles and shrews dived for their escape routes underground. Squirrels leapt from bough to bough, giving cries of alarm. Night birds called warnings. And the Farthing Wood animals held themselves ready, listening to the patter of a thousand rat feet coming closer . . .

'We can catch them in the rear,' Tawny Owl hooted to Holly and Whistler. 'Come on, let's pick them off!'

The three hunting birds, led by Holly, who had first seen the army of rodents, sped up and over the tree-tops. Tawny Owl called to the young owls, his off-spring, as he flew. He knew they were in the woods and he urged them to follow. Soon there were six powerful predators winging their way towards the rear of the rats' columns. The owls flew silently as always. Tawny Owl fumed at the tell-tale whistle from the heron's damaged wing which sounded with every beat. Whistler, racked by pain with every flap of his great grey wings, flew grimly onward in the owls' wake, knowing only too well what Tawny Owl's thoughts would be. But there was no avoiding that regular whistle of air and Owl sensibly forbore to comment.

'There!' hooted Holly as the birds zoomed in only a metre or two above the wood bottom. An involuntary gasp escaped Tawny Owl as he saw the living tide of rats so thickly pressed together that they seemed like one massive creature with countless legs. The odour from the rats' hot bodies fouled the air. It was as though the wood steamed with their rankness.

The young owls began asking what they were to do. They were not yet accomplished hunters and they eyed the mass of rodents with some alarm.

'Take note of our actions,' Tawny Owl told them. 'We're about to swoop. Do as your mother and I do.' He and Holly floated down, their legs dangling, with talons at the ready. Each adult pinpointed a rat, skimmed above it, neatly grasped it without making a landing, then whisked upwards again, each with their catches impaled on their talons. The youngsters perched to watch as once more the parent birds swooped. The rats couldn't avoid the predators. They were so jammed together as they ran that there was nowhere to escape. Again and again the owls picked off their victims, following the running rats, who had no defence against them. Whistler used different tactics. He had no talons, his only weapon his piercing bill. He alighted at the side of the animal mass and stabbed repeatedly as they poured past. One after another fell to the blows from his long beak, which jabbed down like a bayonet. Now the young owls joined the adults, swooping down and then up again, several times missing their mark but practising their movements over and over until they had some measure of skill. They took their toll too, but the rats were so many that the six birds were scarcely able to make an appreciable difference.

By this time the rats were approaching the open ground between the two patches of woodland. The leaders still ran eagerly, unaware of the attacks made on the rear. Bully was caught up in the pace, the speed and the excitement of their advance. He issued no instructions. He was intoxicated by the power of the rodent mass's surge across and he didn't believe any creature could stand in its way.

The Farthing Wood animals heard the increasing din of drumming feet. Fox urged caution. 'We're to stay behind this screen,' he directed the younger foxes, some of whom could barely restrain their eagerness for a fight. 'We're well sheltered and we can attack the rats as they try to pick their way through. I don't want any of you making a charge into the open. You'll be pulled down in a moment.' He stood at the forefront of the motley band of animals. Vixen was by his side and so was Friendly. Behind them Plucky trembled with anticipation. He longed to get to grips with the hated rats. Dash wormed her way through the throng and whispered to him, 'Plucky, don't take any risks. These creatures are dangerous. I couldn't bear it if you got hurt.'

'Don't worry,' he replied. 'I know my duty. Fox is the leader; I'll do as he says.'

The rats broke across the open ground. In the darkness the individual rodents were difficult to see but the friends had no difficulty in detecting the rapid movement of the mass before them. They waited quietly, thinking their own thoughts. Many of them had a score to settle. They remembered Toad and Sinuous. The death of Mossy was as yet unknown to them.

As the invaders approached, the Farthing Wood animals saw with horror the task that faced them. The lines of rats appeared limitless, stretching out into the far distance of the night-clad Park. The sight was awesome. There were quick intakes of breath and little cries of horror, hastily muffled.

'We'll fight to the end,' Fox said quietly. 'We'll save our homes, or die in the attempt. Steady yourselves.'

Bully and Spike got themselves out of the headlong rush, along with some others of Bully's stoutest fighters. They could see where the enemy was gathered behind the sheltering screen of holly. They began to taunt the

animals for their faint-heartedness, but the Farthing
Wood band wouldn't be drawn. The leading rats
crashed against the dense holly scrub, pushed and
urged forward by the serried lines behind. There were
squeals and shrieks of pain as the needle-sharp prickles
lanced their skin. Now the surge slowed a little, allow-
ing the rats to proceed more carefully. The foxes snapped as each rodent tried to force its way through.
Weasel, a furious fighter, attacked a group of three rats
who were endeavouring to thrust themselves between
the end of the holly scrub and the young beech saplings
which grew either side of the prickly screen. Tawny
Owl, Holly and Whistler flew overhead, preparing
themselves to pounce on the flood of scrambling bodies
which smashed through the barrier. The owlets
watched to see what was the next move.

Now the battle began in earnest. The rats opened up
gaps in the holly and swept through, hurling themselves
in clusters at the beleaguered friends. Foxes, rats, owls,
Weasel, Adder, hedgehogs and Whistler were in the
mêlée, fighting tooth and claw with scarcely time to
draw breath. Many of the rats were young and inex-
perienced and were easily crushed, but the big males,
now joined by Bully, Spike and the other champions,
gave a good account of themselves. Female rats too
were in the fight. The Farthing Wood animals were
close to being overwhelmed. Their bodies were covered
by scratching, biting rodents. They tossed them aside,
snapping to left and right, but the sheer weight and
volume of their attackers began to tell.

Frond now ran forward to lend assistance. She could
no longer stand her ground as she watched the ferocity
of the contest. Badger was left unguarded, but even he
heard the fierce sounds of battle raging a short distance
away. He shook himself and lumbered to his set exit.
His friends were sorely pressed, fighting for their lives.

How could he remain outside the battle zone? He didn't wish to survive in a Park devoid of his old companions. He came at a limping run into the heart of the fight, and the savagery of the hateful rats encompassed him too.

Dash and her father raced away from the scene with one thought in their minds: to rouse the rest of the Park's population, deer herd and every willing creature alike, to come to the rescue and to fight side by side to save the Nature Reserve. Now, more than ever before, Dash's blinding speed came into its own. She left her father far behind as she hurtled through the Park, calling in her high-pitched, carrying voice to every beast, every bird, who would listen, begging them to come to the aid of the embattled band of friends. Leveret's message was the same. Whenever he encountered another creature he pleaded with it in the name of White Deer Park to help, to bring others to help.

The messages got through. The entire population of the Reserve had been touched by the menace of the rats. Some had suffered badly, others had watched the rodents' multiplying numbers with fear and alarm. Now the two hares were urging them all to rally round. Predator and prey, carnivore and herbivore began to respond to the plea. They gathered in groups and, seeing other groups assembling nearby, thronged together in their pressing need to liberate themselves and the Park. Dash alerted the white deer, the largest animals in the Reserve. She made them knit together as a herd, stag and hind, by her pressing clarion calls. The herd, with the stags at their head, trotted forward, then broke into a canter. Dash streaked on, crying repeatedly as she criss-crossed the Park. More and more animals swelled the original trickle of nervous contenders into a constant stream. There had never been anything like it in the Park before. The rats were

everyone's enemies and it was as though all the inhabitants of the Reserve had regarded the Farthing Wood
animals as a kind of final bastion against the rodents'
depredations. If these, too, fell before them, each creature realized White Deer Park was doomed. In the air
owls, hawks, crows and magpies – any bird sufficiently
confident in its own size – flew over the tree-tops to the
common destination in the darkness.

Meanwhile the rats were in the ascendancy. Bully
saw the fight as being nearly over. Adder was buried
under a score of rodents as he vainly tried to fasten his
fangs into Spike. Fox, Vixen, Friendly, Plucky and all
the other foxes were twisting and turning, their bodies
encased in clinging, climbing, biting rats, as they continued wearily to snap and lunge at the horde. Their
jaws ached, their limbs shook with fatigue. A few more
moments and they would succumb; their strength was
well-nigh exhausted. Weasel was already on the ground
on his back, kicking and lashing out with tooth and
claw at his assailants. Tawny Owl, Holly and Whistler
continued to make weakened lunges and darts, but the
heron's long legs were being scaled by determined rats
and an escape into flight was now denied him, weighed
down as he was. Frond was still relatively fresh and
battled on grimly, creating a circle of rat corpses
around herself. Badger, who felt any moment he must
draw his last breath, somehow held off the rats who
tried to pull him down. Tawny Owl and Holly flew to
a low branch, utterly spent. They could swoop no more,
their efforts wasted as they saw with the utmost horror
the last of their friends about to be engulfed. They
called to the owlets to take refuge in the highest boughs.

But now the other animals of the Reserve burst upon
the scene, led by the deer herd. The tightly packed
deer trampled across the carpet of rats as they galloped
into the battleground. They left a mat of squirming

bodies behind them, then turned to pound over them again. For the first time, many of the rats fell back, giving the Farthing Wood animals a breathing space. Adder emerged once more into the open and slid out of the path of the deer hoofs. Back came the herd again. The stags lowered their old antlers, which soon would be shed, where the rats were thickest, and swept the rodents up with a toss into the air, from where they fell back to the ground, bruised or maimed. Bully's swagger left him as he saw the tide begin to turn.

At this juncture the first of the other creatures – stoats, weasels, badgers and others eager to lend their support – arrived to tilt the balance further. There were still hundreds of rats as yet unmarked, and now, with the new forces called up by Dash and her father pitching themselves into the struggle, the battle took a different turn. The rats, who had felt they had the upper hand, now found themselves sorely strained as more and more animals arrived while, at the same time, fierce birds made attacks on them from the air.

The embattled Farthing Wood group and their friends took new heart. They found a fresh strength and resolve. The foxes hurled the clinging rats from their coats and, shaking themselves free, plunged into the fray again. Badger and Frond stood together, solid on their feet. Only Weasel now was still in dire straits. The other animals were fully occupied. Suddenly Tawny Owl, who considered himself to be Weasel's last hope, launched a final swoop. He darted down into the midst of the writhing mass of bodies, and claimed two victims with his talons and another with his beak. Weasel was able to clamber back on to his feet. 'Thanks,' he gasped, and the next instant began to fight even more furiously.

Dash and Leveret returned to a scene vastly different from the one which had set them speeding away. The rats were falling back. Bully was squealing orders to retreat before they were all killed. Spike was at last felled by the determined Adder, whose fangs sank into the big rat's hide with an accompanying hiss: 'Sin-u-ousss.'

Fox, free of immediate assailants, sought out Bully. He wanted the mass of rats to lose hope, and the quickest way of achieving this was to deprive them of their leader. He saw the rat scuttling away, out of the thick of the fighting, and gave chase. But another animal was ahead of him. Vixen had remembered her solemn vow to Toad. She fastened herself on Bully and picked him up in her jaws. Then she ran away from the battleground. Bully struggled but Vixen's teeth clamped down more tightly. She ran for the perimeter fence and Fox followed her. They reached the boundary. Vixen clenched her jaws together, tighter and tighter. . . . The helpless Bully was crushed between them. Then Vixen shook the carcass terrier-fashion and tossed it adroitly over the fence beyond White Deer Park. It was a symbolic action.

Fox watched her, grim-faced. 'The others will follow,' he growled.

18

The Park is Saved

The White Deer Park animals, slowly at first, then more swiftly, drove the rats before them. The rodents gave up the fight and ran back to the wood where their comrades, in great agitation and alarm, still clung to the low branches of the trees they had climbed. While the battle raged these latter had waited nervously to play their part in it. They had heard the animal cries – from shrieks and squeals to grunts, barks and growls – and were prepared to drop down on their enemies and finish them off the very moment they were pursued under the trees by the conquering Bully and his troops. They had got themselves so conditioned to this plan that when the defeated rats came running under the trees they automatically leapt on them and began to fight viciously. So rat fought rat in the darkness and many were slaughtered by their own kin before the rodents quite realized what was happening.

Fox and Vixen rushed back to the side of their allies who were still chasing the remnant of the rat horde through the Reserve. Only Badger and Adder stayed behind at the original battleground, congratulating each other on an unexpected victory.

'Well, we survived,' the snake whispered.

'Yes,' Badger panted, 'thanks to the Park's community spirit.'

'You can call it community spirit,' Adder drawled. 'I prefer a more down-to-earth explanation. And that is, that every single inhabitant of this Reserve came to hate the sight of a rat.'

'Sight *and* smell,' Badger muttered distastefully as he glanced around at the heaped rat carcasses. 'Their odour is disgusting. The entire Park is defiled by it.'

As the rats were harried and chased and picked off by their enemies while they tried to escape, their bodies left a trail through White Deer Park. Poor Mossy's remains were hidden by a pile of vanquished rodents. So his death was kept a secret from his friends and, unlike Toad's, his loss could not be mourned. The survivors from the great rat invasion bolted to their runs under the Park's perimeter fence,, through which they had so confidently entered the Reserve weeks before. None of them dared to stay within its boundaries. They thought only of the familiar dark tunnels of the sewer system where, unmolested, they had enjoyed a thriving existence in the past. They found themselves longing for the labyrinth's darkness and its racy fumes. In an hour no rats still breathed within the confines of the Park they had set out to dominate and make their own.

Their pursuers watched their scuttling departure with huge satisfaction. Plucky said to Dash, 'You saved us. You rescued White Deer Park.'

The young hare replied, 'No. It's just that our neighbours responded. But I always knew my great speed was given me for a purpose. When the moment came I had to make use of it.'

The animals, weary but triumphant, dispersed. The deer herd trotted away, their heads held high. The Farthing Wood creatures returned to their own area, as did the other beasts to theirs. Birds greeted the dawn with joyful cries. Together, all of them had rid the Park

of the threat that had hung over it for so long. And, as light began to fill the Nature Reserve again, the true scope of their achievement became apparent. Right across the Park to the boundary fence rat carcasses littered the ground. In some places there were single bodies, in others they were strewn in great numbers. They lay thickest of all where the Farthing Wood animals had taken their stand.

The friends looked at the rodent debris in some awe. 'I never realized before just how numerous they were,' Fox muttered. 'This is an astonishing and a horrible sight.'

'Horrible?' Tawny Owl queried. 'You surely can't be regretting what we've done?'

'Of course not,' Fox answered. 'We've kept the Park free from the risk of disease. But our beloved Reserve is made ugly by this mess of bodies.'

'What should we do?' Frond asked.

'The Warden will take care of things,' Badger told her. 'What a shock he's going to have when he sees all this.'

'Badger, how do you feel?' Fox asked. 'You shouldn't have come to the fight. We thought – '

'Never mind what you thought,' Badger interrupted him. 'You surely know me well enough to realize I wouldn't idle in my set when my friends were facing extinction.'

Fox gave him an affectionate look. 'Dear old Badger. How glad I am we've all come through. Frond, you must cosset him. Badger has proved once again how much we need him.'

Badger was doubly pleased. He knew he hadn't let his old friend down and now he looked forward very much to his cosy arrangement with the young Frond continuing. He had even forgotten about Mossy.

But suddenly Adder said, 'We haven't all come through, Fox. Do we have such short memories?'

Fox looked chastened. Of course Toad was missing from their numbers, and the only possible comfort they could derive from the recent event was that his death had been avenged.

Vixen said, 'We're lucky that more of us weren't killed.'

Now Badger was made to recall his little friend. 'Mole,' he muttered with a puzzled look. 'Where's Mole?'

There was a silence. No-one knew about Mossy but they exchanged glances of distress. They seemed to guess that an accident must have befallen him. Why else wouldn't he have joined them?

'Perhaps he's still in his tunnels,' Badger said feebly. 'I told him to stay underground. But I don't suppose he . . . could remain underground . . . always, could he?' He turned a sorrowful face from one to another of his companions, looking for an expression of hope. There was none offered. Everyone appeared to know Mossy had somehow dropped out of their lives.

'I must discover the truth,' Badger murmured. 'When I'm not so weary I'll . . . I'll. . . .' His voice faded.

'Let me help you back,' Frond whispered. 'You need to rest.'

The young animal's kind voice soothed the old creature and he allowed himself to be escorted back to his set. He certainly was dreadfully tired: tired beyond belief.

'Do you think he'll recover?' Whistler asked. There was a sad tone to his voice.

'On his own, perhaps not,' Vixen murmured. 'But he has Frond now. And she'll try to make sure there's a different outcome.'

The friends, greatly fatigued, made their way to their own dens and nests, exchanging fond words with one another on the way. Before the group had quite broken up Weasel made sure he spoke to Tawny Owl. He had a solemn look about him. 'I say, Owl, I can't let you go before I've properly thanked you.'

Tawny Owl looked at his feet. 'What – what do you mean, Weasel?'

'I mean that – well, I wouldn't be here now if it hadn't been for your action.'

'Oh, I could see you were in difficulties. Say no more about it.' Owl was embarrassed.

'I must say more about it. It was all up with me. You saved me. Why did you do it?'

Tawny Owl started. 'Why? What a strange question. Aren't we supposed to be. . . .'

' "Friends", were you going to say?' Weasel guessed. 'You see, you couldn't quite say it. And that's what's wrong with us two. Because you *are* a friend, Tawny Owl. You've proved it in the best possible way. I don't know why we've always niggled each other. Shall we . . . shall we make a fresh start and try and be more . . . ?'

'Sympathetic?' Owl hazarded.

'Yes.'

'Weasel, I should like that. I really should.'

Badger had been quite right. Later that morning the Warden saw the carnage that had taken place in his preserve overnight. He could scarcely believe his eyes and he tried in vain to picture the tremendous battle which must have taken place. Of course there were not only rat carcasses. Some of their smaller antagonists had also fallen but it was obvious that what had happened illustrated the Park wildlife's will to survive. It was an uplifting example and he marvelled at it. He

quickly organized assistance to clear the unsavoury accumulation of dead animals from the Reserve. When he discovered how they stretched as far as the perimeter fence he knew there had been some sort of wondrous alliance amongst the inhabitants which had determinedly driven the invaders lock, stock and barrel from the sanctuary.

Meanwhile Fox and Vixen were curled up, nose to tail, in their earth. 'Another crisis has come and gone,' said Fox. 'Wouldn't it be a refreshing change if something happened to the Park that would be of benefit to all of us?'

A couple of days later Whistler saw a puzzling sight. As he flew across the edge of the Reserve, returning from a hunting flight, he noticed a new fence, linked to White Deer Park's, was being erected across a portion of the downland. He pondered over the meaning of this but could come to no conclusion and, for the next few days, forgot all about it. Meanwhile rumours, carried by other birds who had also witnessed the construction, spread across the Park. The animals began to dread that the new fence might be connected with some new purge of White Deer Park's inhabitants. They lay low, close to their dens and burrows, but Fox requested Whistler to take a closer look.

'They're enclosing a part of the downland,' he reported after his inspection. 'It's a wide area between here and that other reserve where Weasel and Plucky were taken.'

'A *third* enclosure?' Vixen enquired. 'Whatever can that be for?'

'Perhaps the humans are making it to give Dash an extra long run,' Plucky quipped.

This exhibition of the high spirits which Plucky had

enjoyed ever since being reunited with his friend was deemed to be out of place on this occasion.

'A rather unhelpful remark,' Fox rebuked him.

'Indeed,' said Leveret. 'But what are we to make of this?'

Only Tawny Owl ventured a suggestion. 'It must be for some new kinds of creatures,' he said. 'Some that we haven't seen yet, and who are having their home built first.'

'A nonsensical idea,' remarked Adder.

Weasel, surprisingly, came to Owl's defence. 'Not at all, Adder,' he said. 'Humans never do anything without a purpose. So it must be a home for something.'

'Time will tell,' Adder said drily. 'No point in our playing guessing games.'

The animals dispersed, thinking their own thoughts. None of them felt comfortable with this new development. Then some time later Dash, on one of her madcap races, found herself abruptly in territory she didn't recognize. She halted and looked about her. All at once she realized where she was. She had run directly on to the downland from White Deer Park. She was in the third enclosure! But how had she got there? Running back automatically to the safer confines of the Reserve, she discovered part of the old boundary fence had been removed, so that this new area had been joined on to White Deer Park. She could even see the holes in the ground from which the Park's fence-poles had been removed. Bursting with her news she pelted full-tilt in search of her father.

Leveret's head spun as he heard her gabble. 'Slowly, slowly, Dash,' he pleaded. 'I can't grasp what you're trying to say!'

'The third enclosure *isn't*,' she babbled mysteriously. 'I mean, it isn't a third, it's the *same* enclosure – the

same as ours. It's joined on! Now we can run straight
out on to the downland.'

Leveret stared, his brain registering the information.
'So that's it!' he exclaimed eventually. 'We're all to
have more space!'

'Come and see, Father,' Dash invited him. 'Come
and see how far we can go.'

The naturally cautious Leveret wouldn't commit
himself. 'Well, there's plenty of time for that,' he said.
'I think we should tell the others first.'

Dash stamped her hind feet impatiently. 'You go,'
she replied. 'I can't wait to explore.' And she leapt
away, determined to round up the one animal she knew
would accompany her immediately.

Plucky came to her calls. He was always ready for
play and, when he heard Dash's exciting news, he
didn't lose a moment in agreeing to her proposal. They
ran out together and, at the furthest extent of the new
territory, they discovered another surprise. The
enclosed downland stretched as far as the second sanctuary, whose wall at that point was being breached. A
section of the wall was being knocked down so that
the two parks, connected together by the downland in
between, now made one huge new area. Dash and
Plucky hesitated, scarcely able to credit what they saw.
Of course they kept well back from the men at work.
They couldn't know the complicated human dealings
that had brought about this amazing event. But they
did understand that the two reserves were now united
into one. They and all the animals had a new White
Deer Park, almost double the size of the original. The
two young creatures, overwhelmed by this happy state
of affairs, raced each other back to their friends. Fox's
hope, expressed to Vixen, had been fulfilled.

Soon old friends, removed from the original Reserve

because of over-crowding, were free to return to their habitual homes. Some did. Some didn't. It didn't really matter, though. All the inhabitants were now free to explore the new territory, to enjoy the extra space, to find new homes. Dash exulted in the extension of ground over which she could race her long elastic legs. She and Plucky had plenty of scope for their games now. The Farthing Wood animals went and looked at the new area and liked what they saw. Only Badger showed little interest. Such a distance was too great for him. Of course the friends always returned to the selfsame corner of the Reserve which they had made their home. The Hollow was theirs. They didn't wish to move. Yet they all experienced a new sense of freedom, a new spaciousness in the wonderfully enlarged White Deer Park.

Frond described it to Badger. 'It's a beautiful feeling,' she said, 'to know one's horizons have suddenly been broadened, that none of us need be limited to one small area.'

'I understand,' said Badger as he watched her carrying in some choice grubs and titbits for him. 'But you see, Frond, there will never be anywhere better than this dear familiar spot. Because it's as though we brought our own little piece of Farthing Wood with us.'